Happy Birthday, Lauren!

John Burroughs was a man who loved The Outdoors and I thought you might enjoy his work. He was a very keen observer of lots of things.

Much love, Mom 2022

SIGNS AND SEASONS

BY

JOHN BURROUGHS

BOSTON AND NEW YORK
HOUGHTON, MIFFLIN AND COMPANY
The Riverside Press, Cambridge
1899

Copyright, 1886, 1895,
By JOHN BURROUGHS.

The Riverside Press, Cambridge, Mass., U. S. A.
Electrotyped and Printed by H. O. Houghton & Co.

CONTENTS

SIGNS AND SEASONS

I

A SHARP LOOKOUT

ONE has only to sit down in the woods or fields, or by the shore of the river or lake, and nearly everything of interest will come round to him, — the birds, the animals, the insects; and presently, after his eye has got accustomed to the place, and to the light and shade, he will probably see some plant or flower that he had sought in vain for, and that is a pleasant surprise to him. So, on a large scale, the student and lover of nature has this advantage over people who gad up and down the world, seeking some novelty or excitement; he has only to stay at home and see the procession pass. The great globe swings around to him like a revolving showcase; the change of the seasons is like the passage of strange and new countries; the zones of the earth, with all their beauties and marvels, pass one's door, and linger long in the passing. What a voyage is this we make without leaving for a night our own fireside! St. Pierre well says that a sense of the power and mystery of nature shall

spring up as fully in one's heart after he has made
the circuit of his own field as after returning from
a voyage round the world.   I sit here amid the
junipers of the Hudson, with purpose every year
to go to Florida, or to the West Indies, or to the
Pacific coast, yet the seasons pass and I am still
loitering, 'with a half-defined suspicion, perhaps,
that, if I remain quiet and keep a sharp lookout,
these countries will come to me.   I may stick it
out yet, and not miss much after all.   The great
trouble is for Mohammed to know when the mountain really comes to him.   Sometimes a rabbit or
a jay or a little warbler brings the woods to my
door.   A loon on the river, and the Canada lakes
are here; the sea-gulls and the fish hawk bring the
sea; the call of the wild gander at night, what does
it suggest? and the eagle flapping by, or floating
along on a raft of ice, does not he bring the mountain?   One spring morning five swans flew above
my barn in single file, going northward, — an express train bound for Labrador.   It was a more
exhilarating sight than if I had seen them in their
native haunts.   They made a breeze in my mind,
like a noble passage in a poem.   How gently their
great wings flapped; how easy to fly when spring
gives the impulse!   On another occasion I saw a
line of fowls, probably swans, going northward, at
such a height that they appeared like a faint, waving black line against the sky.   They must have
been at an altitude of two or three miles.   I was
looking intently at the clouds to see which way

they moved, when the birds came into my field of vision. I should never have seen them had they not crossed the precise spot upon which my eye was fixed. As it was near sundown, they were probably launched for an all-night pull. They were going with great speed, and as they swayed a little this way and that, they suggested a slender, all but invisible, aerial serpent cleaving the ether. What a highway was pointed out up there! — an easy grade from the Gulf to Hudson's Bay.

Then the typical spring and summer and autumn days, of all shades and complexions, — one cannot afford to miss any of them; and when looked out upon from one's own spot of earth, how much more beautiful and significant they are! Nature comes home to one most when he is at home; the stranger and traveler finds her a stranger and a traveler also. One's own landscape comes in time to be a sort of outlying part of himself; he has sowed himself broadcast upon it, and it reflects his own moods and feelings; he is sensitive to the verge of the horizon: cut those trees, and he bleeds; mar those hills, and he suffers. How has the farmer planted himself in his fields; builded himself into his stone walls, and evoked the sympathy of the hills by his struggle! This home feeling, this domestication of nature, is important to the observer. This is the bird-lime with which he catches the bird; this is the private door that admits him behind the scenes. This is one source of Gilbert White's charm, and of the charm of Thoreau's "Walden."

The birds that come about one's door in winter, or that build in his trees in summer, what a peculiar interest they have! What crop have I sowed in Florida or in California, that I should go there to reap? I should be only a visitor, or formal caller upon nature, and the family would all wear masks. No; the place to observe nature is where you are; the walk to take to-day is the walk you took yesterday. You will not find just the same things: both the observed and the observer have changed; the ship is on another tack in both cases.

I shall probably never see another just such day as yesterday was, because one can never exactly repeat his observation, — cannot turn the leaf of the book of life backward, — and because each day has characteristics of its own. This was a typical March day, clear, dry, hard, and windy, the river rumpled and crumpled, the sky intense, distant objects strangely near; a day full of strong light, unusual; an extraordinary lightness and clearness all around the horizon, as if there were a diurnal aurora streaming up and burning through the sunlight; smoke from the first spring fires rising up in various directions; a day that winnowed the air, and left no film in the sky. At night, how the big March bellows did work! Venus was like a great lamp in the sky. The stars all seemed brighter than usual, as if the wind blew them up like burning coals. Venus actually seemed to flare in the wind.

Each day foretells the next, if one could read the

signs; to-day is the progenitor of to-morrow. When
the atmosphere is telescopic, and distant objects
stand out unusually clear and sharp, a storm is near.
We are on the crest of the wave, and the depression
follows quickly. It often happens that clouds are
not so indicative of a storm as the total absence of
clouds. In this state of the atmosphere the stars
are unusually numerous and bright at night, which
is also a bad omen.

I find this observation confirmed by Humboldt.
"It appears," he says, "that the transparency of
the air is prodigiously increased when a certain
quantity of water is uniformly diffused through it."
Again, he says that the mountaineers of the Alps
"predict a change of weather when, the air being
calm, the Alps covered with perpetual snow seem
on a sudden to be nearer the observer, and their
outlines are marked with great distinctness on the
azure sky." He further observes that the same
condition of the atmosphere renders distant sounds
more audible.

There is one redness in the east in the morning
that means storm, another that means wind. The
former is broad, deep, and angry; the clouds look
like a huge bed of burning coals just raked open;
the latter is softer, more vapory, and more widely
extended. Just at the point where the sun is going
to rise, and some minutes in advance of his coming,
there sometimes rises straight upward a rosy column;
it is like a shaft of deeply dyed vapor, blending
with and yet partly separated from the clouds, and

the base of which presently comes to glow like the
sun itself. The day that follows is pretty certain
to be very windy. At other times the under sides
of the eastern clouds are all turned to pink or rose-
colored wool; the transformation extends until
nearly the whole sky flushes, even the west glowing
slightly; the sign is always to be interpreted as
meaning fair weather.

The approach of great storms is seldom heralded
by any striking or unusual phenomenon. The real
weather gods are free from brag and bluster; but
the sham gods fill the sky with portentous signs and
omens. I recall one 5th of March as a day that
would have filled the ancient observers with dread-
ful forebodings. At ten o'clock the sun was attended by four extraordinary sun-dogs. A large
bright halo encompassed him, on the top of which
the segment of a larger circle rested, forming a sort
of heavy brilliant crown. At the bottom of the
circle, and depending from it, was a mass of soft,
glowing, iridescent vapor. On either side, like
fragments of the larger circle, were two brilliant
arcs. Altogether, it was the most portentous storm-
breeding sun I ever beheld. In a dark hemlock
wood in a valley, the owls were hooting ominously,
and the crows dismally cawing. Before night the
storm set in, a little sleet and rain of a few hours'
duration, insignificant enough compared with the
signs and wonders that preceded it.

To what extent the birds or animals can foretell
the weather is uncertain. When the swallows are

seen hawking very high it is a good indication; the insects upon which they feed venture up there only in the most auspicious weather. Yet bees will continue to leave the hive when a storm is imminent. I am told that one of the most reliable weather signs they have down in Texas is afforded by the ants. The ants bring their eggs up out of their underground retreats and expose them to the warmth of the sun to be hatched. When they are seen carrying them in again in great haste, though there be not a cloud in the sky, your walk or your drive must be postponed: a storm is at hand. There is a passage in Virgil that is doubtless intended to embody a similar observation, though none of his translators seem to have hit its meaning accurately: —

> " Sæpius et tectis penetralibus extulit ova
> Angustum formica terens iter: "

"Often also has the pismire making a narrow road brought forth her eggs out of the hidden recesses" is the literal translation of old John Martyn.

> " Also the ant, incessantly traveling
> The same straight way with the eggs of her hidden store,"

is one of the latest metrical translations. Dryden has it: —

> " The careful ant her secret cell forsakes
> And drags her eggs along the narrow tracks,"

which comes nearer to the fact. When a storm is coming, Virgil also makes his swallows skim low about the lake, which agrees with the observation above.

The critical moments of the day as regards the
weather are at sunrise and sunset. A clear sunset
is always a good sign; an obscured sun, just at the
moment of going down after a bright day, bodes
storm. There is much truth, too, in the saying
that if it rain before seven, it will clear before
eleven. Nine times in ten it will turn out thus.
The best time for it to begin to rain or snow, if it
wants to hold out, is about mid-forenoon. The
great storms usually begin at this time. On all
occasions the weather is very sure to declare itself
before eleven o'clock. If you are going on a pic-
nic, or are going to start on a journey, and the
morning is unsettled, wait till ten and one half
o'clock, and you shall know what the remainder
of the day will be. Midday clouds and afternoon
clouds, except in the season of thunderstorms, are
usually harmless idlers and vagabonds. But more
to be relied on than any obvious sign is that subtle
perception of the condition of the weather which
a man has who spends much of his time in the
open air. He can hardly tell how he knows it is
going to rain; he hits the fact as an Indian does
the mark with his arrow, without calculating and
by a kind of sure instinct. As you read a man's
purpose in his face, so you learn to read the purpose of the weather in the face of the day.

In observing the weather, however, as in the
diagnosis of disease, the diathesis is all-important.
All signs fail in a drought, because the predisposi-
tion, the diathesis, is so strongly toward fair wea-

ther; and the opposite signs fail during a wet spell, because nature is caught in the other rut.

Observe the lilies of the field. Sir John Lubbock says the dandelion lowers itself after flowering, and lies close to the ground while it is maturing its seed, and then rises up. It is true that the dandelion lowers itself after flowering, retires from society, as it were, and meditates in seclusion; but after it lifts itself up again the stalk begins anew to grow, it lengthens daily, keeping just above the grass till the fruit is ripened, and the little globe of silvery down is carried many inches higher than was the ring of golden flowers. And the reason is obvious. The plant depends upon the wind to scatter its seeds; every one of these little vessels spreads a sail to the breeze, and it is necessary that they be launched above the grass and weeds, amid which they would be caught and held did the stalk not continue to grow and outstrip the rival vegetation. It is a curious instance of foresight in a weed.

I wish I could read as clearly this puzzle of the button-balls (American plane-tree). Why has Nature taken such particular pains to keep these balls hanging to the parent tree intact till spring? What secret of hers has she buttoned in so securely? for these buttons will not come off. The wind cannot twist them off, nor warm nor wet hasten or retard them. The stem, or peduncle, by which the ball is held in the fall and winter, breaks up into a dozen or more threads or strands, that are stronger

than those of hemp. When twisted tightly they make a little cord that I find it impossible to break with my hands. Had they been longer, the Indian would surely have used them to make his bow-strings and all the other strings he required. One could hang himself with a small cord of them. (In South America, Humboldt saw excellent cordage made by the Indians from the petioles of the Chi-quichiqui palm.) Nature has determined that these buttons should stay on. In order that the seeds of this tree may germinate, it is probably necessary that they be kept dry during the winter, and reach the ground after the season of warmth and moisture is fully established. In May, just as the leaves and the new balls are emerging, at the touch of a warm, moist south wind, these spherical packages suddenly go to pieces — explode, in fact, like tiny bombshells that were fused to carry to this point — and scatter their seeds to the four winds. They yield at the same time a fine pollen-like dust that one would suspect played some part in fertilizing the new balls, did not botany teach him otherwise. At any rate, it is the only deciduous tree I know of that does not let go the old seed till the new is well on the way. It is plain why the sugar-berry-tree or lotus holds its drupes all winter: it is in order that the birds may come and sow the seed. The berries are like small gravel stones with a sugar coating, and a bird will not eat them till he is pretty hard pressed, but in late fall and winter the robins, cedar-birds, and bluebirds devour them

readily, and of course lend their wings to scatter the seed far and wide. The same is true of juniper-berries, and the fruit of the bitter-sweet.

In certain other cases where the fruit tends to hang on during the winter, as with the bladder-nut and the honey-locust, it is probably because the frost and the perpetual moisture of the ground would rot or kill the germ. To beechnuts, chestnuts, and acorns the moisture of the ground and the covering of leaves seem congenial, though too much warmth and moisture often cause the acorns to germinate prematurely. I have found the ground under the oaks in December covered with nuts, all anchored to the earth by purple sprouts. But the winter which follows such untimely growths generally proves fatal to them.

One must always cross-question nature if he would get at the truth, and he will not get at it then unless he frames his questions with great skill. Most persons are unreliable observers because they put only leading questions, or vague questions.

Perhaps there is nothing in the operations of nature to which we can properly apply the term intelligence, yet there are many things that at first sight look like it. Place a tree or plant in an unusual position and it will prove itself equal to the occasion, and behave in an unusual manner; it will show original resources; it will seem to try intelligently to master the difficulties. Up by Furlow Lake, where I was camping out, a young hemlock had become established upon the end of a

large and partly decayed log that reached many feet
out into the lake. The young tree was eight or
nine feet high; it had sent its roots down into the
log and clasped it around on the outside, and had
apparently discovered that there was water instead
of soil immediately beneath it, and that its sustenance must be sought elsewhere and that quickly.
Accordingly it had started one large root, by far
the largest of all, for the shore along the top of the
log. This root, when I saw the tree, was six or
seven feet long, and had bridged more than half the
distance that separated the tree from the land.

Was this a kind of intelligence? If the shore
had lain in the other direction, no doubt at all but
the root would have started for the other side. I
know a yellow pine that stands on the side of a
steep hill. To make its position more secure, it
has thrown out a large root at right angles with its
stem directly into the bank above it, which acts as
a stay or guy-rope. It was positively the best
thing the tree could do. The earth has washed
away so that the root where it leaves the tree is
two feet above the surface of the soil.

Yet both these cases are easily explained, and
without attributing any power of choice, or act of
intelligent selection, to the trees. In the case of
the little hemlock upon the partly submerged log,
roots were probably thrown out equally in all directions; on all sides but one they reached the water
and stopped growing; the water checked them; but
on the land side, the root on the top of the log, not

meeting with any obstacle of the kind, kept on growing, and thus pushing its way toward the shore. It was a case of survival, not of the fittest, but of that which the situation favored, — the fittest with reference to position.

So with the pine-tree on the side of the hill. It probably started its roots in all directions, but only the one on the upper side survived and matured. Those on the lower side finally perished, and others lower down took their places. Thus the whole life upon the globe, as we see it, is the result of this blind groping and putting forth of Nature in every direction, with failure of some of her ventures and the success of others, the circumstances, the environments, supplying the checks and supplying the stimulus, the seed falling upon the barren places just the same as upon the fertile. No discrimination on the part of Nature that we can express in the terms of our own consciousness, but ceaseless experiments in every possible direction. The only thing inexplicable is the inherent impulse to experiment, the original push, the principle of Life.

The good observer of nature holds his eye long and firmly to the point, as one does when looking at a puzzle picture, and will not be baffled. The cat catches the mouse, not merely because she watches for him, but because she is armed to catch him and is quick. So the observer finally gets the fact, not only because he has patience, but because his eye is sharp and his inference swift. Many a shrewd old farmer looks upon the milky way as a kind of weathercock, and will tell you that the way it points at night indicates the direction of the wind the following day. So, also, every new moon is either a dry moon or a wet moon, dry if a powder-horn would hang upon the lower limb, wet if it would not; forgetting the fact that, as a rule, when it is dry in one part of the continent it is wet in some other part, and *vice versa.* When he kills his hogs in the fall, if the pork be very hard and solid he predicts a severe winter; if soft and loose, the opposite; again overlooking the fact that the kind of food and the temperature of the fall make the pork hard or make it soft. So with a hundred other signs, all the result of hasty and incomplete observations.

One season, the last day of December was very warm. The bees were out of the hive, and there was no frost in the air or in the ground. I was walking in the woods, when as I paused in the shade of a hemlock-tree I heard a sound proceed from beneath the wet leaves. on the ground but a few feet from me that suggested a frog. Following it cautiously up, I at last determined upon the exact spot from whence the sound issued; lifting up the thick layer of leaves, there sat a frog — the wood frog, one of the first to appear in the marshes in spring, and which I have elsewhere called the "clucking frog" — in a little excavation in the surface of the leaf mould. As it sat there the top of its back was level with the surface of the ground. This, then, was its hibernaculum; here it was prepared to pass the winter, with only a coverlid of wet matted leaves between it and zero weather. Forthwith I set up as a prophet of warm weather, and among other things predicted a failure of the ice crop on the river; which, indeed, others, who had not heard frogs croak on the 31st of December, had also begun to predict. Surely, I thought, this frog knows what it is about; here is the wisdom of nature; it would have gone deeper into the ground than that if a severe winter was approaching; so I was not anxious about my coal-bin, nor disturbed by longings for Florida. But what a winter followed, the winter of 1885, when the Hudson became coated with ice nearly two feet thick, and when March was as cold as January! I thought of my frog under the hemlock and wondered how it was faring. So one day the latter part of March, when the snow was gone, and there was a feeling of spring in the air, I turned aside in my walk to investigate it. The matted leaves were still frozen hard, but I succeeded in lifting them up and exposing the frog. There it sat as fresh and unscathed as in the fall. The ground beneath and all about it was still frozen like a rock, but apparently it had some means of its own of resisting the frost. It winked and bowed its head when I touched it, but did not seem inclined to leave its retreat. Some days later, after the frost was nearly all out of the ground, I passed that way, and found my frog had come out of its seclusion and was resting amid the dry leaves. There was not much jump in it yet, but its color was growing lighter. A few more warm days, and its fellows, and doubtless itself too, were croaking and gamboling in the marshes.

This incident convinced me of two things; namely, that frogs know no more about the coming weather than we do, and that they do not retreat as deep into the ground to pass the winter as has been supposed. I used to think the muskrats could foretell an early and a severe winter, and have so written. But I am now convinced they cannot; they know as little about it as I do. Sometimes on an early and severe frost they seem to get alarmed and go to building their houses, but usually they seem to build early or late, high or low, just as the whim takes them.

In most of the operations of nature there is at least one unknown quantity; to find the exact value of this unknown factor is not so easy. The wool of the sheep, the fur of the animals, the feathers of the fowls, the husks of the maize, why are they thicker some seasons than others; what is the value of the unknown quantity here? Does it indicate a severe winter approaching? Only observations extending over a series of years could determine the point. How much patient observation it takes to settle many of the facts in the lives of the birds, animals, and insects! Gilbert White was all his life trying to determine whether or not swallows passed the winter in a torpid state in the mud at the bottom of ponds and marshes, and he died ignorant of the truth that they do not. Do honey-bees injure the grape and other fruits by puncturing the skin for the juice? The most patient watching by many skilled eyes all over the country has not yet settled the point. For my own part, I am convinced that they do not. The honey-bee is not the rough-and-ready freebooter that the wasp and bumblebee are; she has somewhat of feminine timidity, and leaves the first rude assaults to them. I knew the honey-bee was very fond of the locust blossoms, and that the trees hummed like a hive in the height of their flowering, but I did not know that the bumblebee was ever the sapper and miner that went ahead in this enterprise, till one day I placed myself amid the foliage of a locust and saw him savagely bite through the shank of the flower and extract the nectar, followed by a honey-bee that in every instance searched for this opening, and probed long and carefully for the leavings of her burly purveyor. The bumblebee rifles the dicentra and the columbine of their treasures in the same manner, namely, by slitting their pockets from the outside, and the honey-bee gleans after him, taking the small change he leaves. In the case of the locust, however, she usually obtains the honey without the aid of the larger bee.

Speaking of the honey-bee reminds me that the subtle and sleight-of-hand manner in which she fills her baskets with pollen and propolis is characteristic of much of Nature's doings. See the bee going from flower to flower with the golden pellets on her thighs, slowly and mysteriously increasing in *[text partially illegible]* ... If the miller were to make the mill if the ... is made by gathering the particles of flour from ... and ... he must rapidly about ... dusting them in his pockets, he would be doing pretty nearly what the bee does. The little miller knows covered with the pollen of the flower, and soon, while on the wing, brushes it off with the hair brush on certain of her feet, and by some jugglery or clever science it is in her pollen basket. One needs to look long and intently to see through the trick. Many says they fill their baskets with their hind feet, and that they fill their fore feet with their trunks, but it is a much more subtle operation than this. I have seen the bees come to a meal barrel in early spring, and to a pile of hardwood sawdust before there was yet anything in nature for them to work upon, and, having dusted their coats with the finer particles of the meal or the sawdust, hover on the wing above the mass till the little legerdemain feat is performed. Nature fills her baskets by the same sleight-of-hand, and the observer must be on the alert who would possess her secret. If the ancients had looked a little closer and sharper, would they ever have believed in spontaneous generation in the superficial way in which they did; that maggots, for instance, were generated spontaneously in putrid flesh? Could they not see the spawn of the blow-flies? Or, if Virgil had been a real observer of the bees, would he ever have credited, as he certainly appears to do, the fable of bees originating from the carcass of a steer?

or that on windy days they carried little stones for
ballast? or that two hostile swarms fought each
other in the air? Indeed, the ignorance, or the
false science, of the ancient observers, with regard
to the whole subject of bees, is most remarkable;
not false science merely with regard to their more
hidden operations, but with regard to that which is
open and patent to all who have eyes in their heads,
and have ever had to do with them. And Pliny
names authors who had devoted their whole lives
to the study of the subject.

But the ancients, like women and children, were
not accurate observers. Just at the critical moment
their eyes were unsteady, or their fancy, or their
credulity, or their impatience, got the better of
them, so that their science was half fact and half
fable. Thus, for instance, because the young cuckoo
at times appeared to take the head of its small fos-
ter mother quite into its mouth while receiving its
food, they believed that it finally devoured her.
Pliny, who embodied the science of his times in
his natural history, says of the wasp that it carries
spiders to its nest, and then sits upon them until it
hatches its young from them. A little careful
observation would have shown him that this was
only a half truth; that the whole truth was, that
the spiders were entombed with the egg of the wasp
to serve as food for the young when the egg shall
have hatched.

What curious questions Plutarch discusses, as,
for instance, "What is the reason that a bucket of

water drawn out of a well, if it stands all night in the air that is in the well, is more cold in the morning than the rest of the water?" He could probably have given many reasons why "a watched pot never boils." The ancients, the same author says, held that the bodies of those killed by lightning never putrefy; that the sight of a ram quiets an enraged elephant; that a viper will lie stock still if touched by a beechen leaf; that a wild bull grows tame if bound with the twigs of a fig-tree; that a hen purifies herself with straw after she has laid an egg; that the deer buries his cast-off horns; that a goat stops the whole herd by holding a branch of the sea-holly in his mouth, etc. They sought to account for such things without stopping to ask, Are they true? Nature was too novel, or else too fearful, to them to be deliberately pursued and hunted down. Their youthful joy in her, or their dread and awe in her presence, may be better than our scientific satisfaction, or cool wonder, or our vague, mysterious sense of "something far more deeply interfused;" yet we cannot change with them if we would, and I, for one, would not if I could. Science does not mar nature. The railroad, Thoreau found, after all, to be about the wildest road he knew of, and the telegraph wires the best æolian harp out of doors. Study of nature deepens the mystery and the charm because it removes the horizon farther off. We cease to fear, perhaps, but how can one cease to marvel and to love?

The fields and woods and waters about one are

a book from which he may draw exhaustless enter-
tainment, if he will. One must not only learn
the writing, he must translate the language, the
signs, and the hieroglyphics. It is a very quaint
and elliptical writing, and much must be supplied
by the wit of the translator. At any rate, the les-
son is to be well conned. Gilbert White said that
that locality would be found the richest in zoölogi-
cal or botanical specimens which was most thoroughly examined. For more than forty years he
studied the ornithology of his district without ex-
hausting the subject. I thought I knew my own
tramping ground pretty well, but one April day,
when I looked a little closer than usual into a small
semi-stagnant lakelet where I had peered a hundred
times before, I suddenly discovered scores of little
creatures that were as new to me as so many nymphs
would have been. They were partly fish-shaped,
from an inch to an inch and a half long, semi-trans-
parent, with a dark brownish line visible the entire
length of them (apparently the thread upon which
the life of the animal hung, and by which its all
but impalpable frame was held together), and sus-
pending themselves in the water, or impelling themselves swiftly forward by means of a double row of
fine, waving, hair-like appendages, that arose from
what appeared to be the back, — a kind of undulating, pappus-like wings. What was it? I did not
know. None of my friends or scientific acquaint-
ances knew. I wrote to a learned man, an authority upon fish, describing the creature as well as I

appears to start in several things simultaneously.
Of a warm thawy day in February the snow is
suddenly covered with myriads of snow fleas looking like black, new powder just spilled there.   Or
you may see a winged insect in the air.   On the
selfsame day the grass in the spring run and the
catkins on the alders will have started a little; and
if you look sharply, while passing along some sheltered nook or grassy slope where the sunshine lies
warm on the bare ground, you will probably see a
grasshopper or two.   The grass hatches out under
the snow, and why should not the grasshopper?
At any rate, a few such hardy specimens may be
found in the latter part of our milder winters
wherever the sun has uncovered a sheltered bit of
grass for a few days, even after a night of ten or
twelve degrees of frost.   Take them in the shade,
and let them freeze stiff as pokers, and when thawed
out again they will hop briskly.   And yet, if a poet
were to put grasshoppers in his winter poem, we
should require pretty full specifications of him, or
else fur to clothe them with.   Nature will not be
cornered, yet she does many things in a corner and
surreptitiously.   She is all things to all men; she
has whole truths, half truths, and quarter truths, if
not still smaller fractions.   The careful observer
finds this out sooner or later.   Old fox-hunters will
tell you, on the evidence of their own eyes, that
there is a black fox and a silver-gray fox, two
species, but there are not; the black fox is black
when coming toward you or running from you, and

silver gray at point-blank view, when the eye penetrates the fur; each separate hair is gray the first half and black the last. This is a sample of nature's half truths.

Which are our sweet-scented wild flowers? Put your nose to every flower you pluck, and you will be surprised how your list will swell the more you smell. I plucked some wild blue violets one day, the *ovata* variety of the *sagittata*, that had a faint perfume of sweet clover, but I never could find another that had any odor. A pupil disputed with his teacher about the hepatica, claiming in opposition that it was sweet-scented. Some hepaticas are sweet-scented and some are not, and the perfume is stronger some seasons than others. After the unusually severe winter of 1880–81, the variety of hepatica called the sharp-lobed was markedly sweet in nearly every one of the hundreds of specimens I examined. A handful of them exhaled a most delicious perfume. The white ones that season were largely in the ascendant; and probably the white specimens of both varieties, one season with another, will oftenest prove sweet-scented. Darwin says a considerably larger proportion of white flowers are sweet-scented than of any other color. The only sweet violets I can depend upon are white, *Viola blanda* and *Viola Canadensis*, and white largely predominates among our other odorous wild flowers. All the fruit-trees have white or pinkish blossoms. I recall no native blue flower of New York or New England that is fragrant except in the

rare case of the arrow-leaved violet, above referred
to. The earliest yellow flowers, like the dandelion
and yellow violets, are not fragrant. Later in the
season yellow is frequently accompanied with fragrance, as in the evening primrose, the yellow lady's-
slipper, horned bladderwort, and others.

My readers probably remember that on a former
occasion I have mildly taken the poet Bryant to
task for leading his readers to infer that the early
yellow violet was sweet-scented. In view of the
capriciousness of the perfume of certain of our wild
flowers, I have during the past few years tried
industriously to convict myself of error in respect
to this flower. The round-leaved yellow violet was
one of the earliest and most abundant wild flowers
in the woods where my youth was passed, and
whither I still make annual pilgrimages. I have
pursued it on mountains and in lowlands, in
"beechen woods" and amid the hemlocks; and
while, with respect to its earliness, it overtakes the
hepatica in the latter part of April, as do also the
dog's-tooth violet and the claytonia, yet the first
hepaticas, where the two plants grow side by side,
bloom about a week before the first violet. And I
have yet to find one that has an odor that could be
called a perfume. A handful of them, indeed, has
a faint, bitterish smell, not unlike that of the dandelion in quality; but if every flower that has a
smell is sweet-scented, then every bird that makes
a noise is a songster.

On the occasion above referred to, I also dissented from Lowell's statement, in "Al Fresco," that in early summer the dandelion blooms, in general, with the buttercup and the clover. I am aware that such criticism of the poets is small game, and not worth the powder. General truth, and not specific fact, is what we are to expect of the poets. Bryant's "Yellow Violet" poem is tender and appropriate, and such as only a real lover and observer of nature could feel or express; and Lowell's "Al Fresco" is full of the luxurious feeling of early summer, and this is, of course, the main thing; a good reader cares for little else; I care for little else myself. But when you take your coin to the assay office it must be weighed and tested, and in the comments referred to I (unwisely perhaps) sought to smelt this gold of the poets in the naturalist's pot, to see what alloy of error I could detect in it. Were the poems true to their last word? They were not, and much subsequent investigation has only confirmed my first analysis. The general truth is on my side, and the specific fact, if such exists in this case, on the side of the poets. It is possible that there may be a fragrant yellow violet, as an exceptional occurrence, like that of the sweet-scented, arrow-leaved species above referred to, and that in some locality it may have bloomed before the hepatica; also that Lowell may have seen a belated dandelion or two in June, amid the clover and the buttercups; but, if so, they were the exception, and not the rule, — the specific or accidental fact, and not the general truth.

Dogmatism about nature, or about anything else, very often turns out to be an ungrateful cur that bites the hand that reared it. I speak from experience. I was once quite certain that the honey-bee did not work upon the blossoms of the trailing arbutus, but while walking in the woods one April day I came upon a spot of arbutus swarming with honey-bees. They were so eager for it that they crawled under the leaves and the moss to get at the blossoms, and refused on the instant the hive-honey which I happened to have with me, and which I offered them. I had had this flower under observation more than twenty years, and had never before seen it visited by honey-bees. The same season I saw them for the first time working upon the flower of bloodroot and of adder's-tongue. Hence I would not undertake to say again what flowers bees do not work upon. Virgil implies that they work upon the violet, and for aught I know they may. I have seen them very busy on the blossoms of the white oak, though this is not considered a honey or pollen yielding tree. From the smooth sumac they reap a harvest in midsummer, and in March they get a good grist of pollen from the skunk-cabbage.

I presume, however, it would be safe to say that there is a species of smilax with an unsavory name that the bee does not visit, *herbacea*. The production of this plant is a curious freak of nature. I find it growing along the fences where one would look for wild roses or the sweetbrier; its recurving or climbing stem, its glossy, deep-green, heart-shaped leaves, its clustering umbels of small green-ish yellow flowers, making it very pleasing to the eye; but to examine it closely one must positively hold his nose. It would be too cruel a joke to offer it to any person not acquainted with it to smell. It is like the vent of a charnel-house. It is first cousin to the trilliums, among the prettiest of our native wild flowers, and the same bad blood crops out in the purple trillium or birthroot.

Nature will include the disagreeable and repulsive also. I have seen the phallic fungus growing in June under a rosebush. There was the rose, and beneath it, springing from the same mould, was this diabolical offering to Priapus. With the perfume of the roses into the open window came the stench of this hideous parody, as if in mockery. I removed it, and another appeared in the same place shortly afterward. The earthman was rampant and insulting. Pan is not dead yet. At least he still makes a ghastly sign here and there in nature.

The good observer of nature exists in fragments, a trait here and a trait there. Each person sees what it concerns him to see. The fox-hunter knows pretty well the ways and habits of the fox, but on any other subject he is apt to mislead you. He comes to see only fox traits in whatever he looks upon. The bee-hunter will follow the bee, but lose the bird. The farmer notes what affects his crops and his earnings, and little else. Common people, St. Pierre says, observe without reasoning, and the learned reason without observing. If one could apply to the observation of nature the sense and skill of the South American *rastreador*, or trailer, how much he would track home! This man's eye, according to the accounts of travelers, is keener than a hound's scent. A fugitive can no more elude him than he can elude fate. His perceptions are said to be so keen that the displacement of a leaf or pebble, or the bending down of a spear of grass, or the removal of a little dust from the fence are enough to give him the clew. He sees the half-obliterated footprints of a thief in the sand, and carries the impression in his eye till a year afterward, when he again detects the same footprint in the suburbs of a city, and the culprit is tracked home and caught. I knew a man blind from his youth who not only went about his own neighborhood without a guide, turning up to his neighbor's gate or door as unerringly as if he had the best of eyes, but who would go many miles on an errand to a new part of the country. He seemed to carry a map of the township in the bottom of his feet, a most minute and accurate survey. He never took the wrong road and he knew the right house when he had reached it. He was a miller and fuller, and ran his mill at night while his sons ran it by day. He never made a mistake with his customers' bags or wool, knowing each man's by the sense of touch. He frightened a colored man whom he detected stealing, as if he had seen out of the back of his head. Such facts show one how deli-

cate and sensitive a man's relation to outward
nature through his bodily senses may become.
Heighten it a little more, and he could forecast the
weather and the seasons, and detect hidden springs
and minerals. A good observer has something of
this delicacy and quickness of perception. All the
great poets and naturalists have it. Agassiz traces
the glaciers like a *rastreador;* and Darwin misses
no step that the slow but tireless gods of physical
change have taken, no matter how they cross or
retrace their course. In the obscure fish-worm he
sees an agent that has kneaded and leavened the soil
like giant hands.

One secret of success in observing nature is capacity to take a hint; a hair may show where a
lion is hid. One must put this and that together,
and value bits and shreds. Much alloy exists with
the truth. The gold of nature does not look like
gold at the first glance. It must be smelted and
refined in the mind of the observer. And one
must crush mountains of quartz and wash hills of
sand to get it. To know the indications is the
main matter. People who do not know the secret
are eager to take a walk with the observer' to find
where the mine is that contains such nuggets, little
knowing that his ore-bed is but a gravel-heap to
them. How insignificant appear most of the facts
which one sees in his walks, in the life of the
birds, the flowers, the animals, or in the phases of
the landscape, or the look of the sky! — insignificant until they are put through some mental or

emotional process and their true value appears.
The diamond looks like a pebble until it is cut.
One goes to Nature only for hints and half truths.
Her facts are crude until you have absorbed them
or translated them.   Then the ideal steals in and
lends a charm in spite of one.   It is not so much
what we see as what the thing seen suggests.   We
all see about the same; to one it means much, to
another little.   A fact that has passed through the
mind of man, like lime or iron that has passed
through his blood, has some quality or property
superadded or brought out that it did not possess
before.   You may go to the fields and the woods,
and gather fruit that is ripe for the palate without
any aid of yours, but you cannot do this in science
or in art.   Here truth must be disentangled and
interpreted, — must be made in the image of man.
Hence all good observation is more or less a refining
and transmuting process, and the secret is to know
the crude material when you see it.   I think of
Wordsworth's lines: —

> "The mighty world
> Of eye and ear, both what they half create, and what perceive; "

which is as true in the case of the naturalist as of
the poet; both "half create " the world they describe.
Darwin does something to his facts as well as Tennyson to his.   Before a fact can become poetry, it
must pass through the heart or the imagination of
the poet; before it can become science, it must pass
through the understanding of the scientist.   Or one
may say, it is with the thoughts and half thoughts

that the walker gathers in the woods and fields, as with the common weeds and coarser wild flowers which he plucks for a bouquet, — wild carrot, purple aster, moth mullein, sedge, grass, etc. : they look common and uninteresting enough there in the fields, but the moment he separates them from the tangled mass, and brings them indoors, and places them in a vase, say of some choice glass, amid artificial things, — behold, how beautiful! They have an added charm and significance at once; they are defined and identified, and what was common and familiar becomes unexpectedly attractive. The writer's style, the quality of mind he brings, is the vase in which his commonplace impressions and incidents are made to appear so beautiful and significant.

Man can have but one interest in nature, namely, to see himself reflected or interpreted there, and we quickly neglect both poet and philosopher who fail to satisfy, in some measure, this feeling.

II

A SPRAY OF PINE

HOW different the expression of the pine, in fact of all the coniferæ, from that of the deciduous trees! Not different merely by reason of color and foliage, but by reason of form. The deciduous trees have greater diversity of shapes; they tend to branch endlessly; they divide and sub-divide until the original trunk is lost in a maze of limbs. Not so the pine and its congeners. Here the main thing is the central shaft; there is one dominant shoot which leads all the rest, and which points the tree upward; the original type is never departed from: the branches shoot out at nearly right angles to the trunk, and occur in regular whorls; the main stem is never divided unless some accident nips the leading shoot, when two secondary branches will often rise up and lead the tree for-ward. The pine has no power to develop new buds, new shoots, like the deciduous trees; no power of spontaneous variation to meet new exi-gencies, new requirements. It is, as it were, cast in a mould. Its buds, its branches occur in regu-lar series and after a regular pattern. Interrupt this series, try to vary this pattern, and the tree

is powerless to adapt itself to any other. Victor
Hugo, in his old age, compared himself to a tree
that had been many times cut down, but which
always sprouted again. But the pines do not sprout
again. The spontaneous development of a new bud
or a new shoot rarely or never occurs. The hemlock seems to be under the same law. I have cut
away all the branches, and rubbed away all the
buds, of a young sapling of this species, and found
the tree, a year and a half later, full of life, but
with no leaf or bud upon it. It could not break
the spell. One bud would have released it and set
its currents going again, but it was powerless to develop it. Remove the bud, or the new growth
from the end of the central shaft of the branch
of a pine, and in a year or two the branch will
die back to the next joint; remove the whorl of
branches here and it will die back to the next
whorl, and so on.

When you cut the top of a pine or a spruce,
removing the central and leading shaft, the tree
does not develop and send forth a new one to take
the place of the old, but a branch from the next in
rank, that is, from the next whorl of limbs, is promoted to take the lead. It is curious to witness
this limb rise up and get into position. One season
I cut off the tops of some young hemlocks that
were about ten feet high, that I had balled in the
winter and had moved into position for a hedge.
The next series of branches consisted of three that
shot out nearly horizontally. As time passed, one

of these branches, apparently the most vigorous, began to lift itself up very slowly toward the place occupied by the lost leader. The third year it stood at an angle of about forty-five degrees; the fourth year it had gained about half the remaining distance, when the clipping shears again cut it down. In five years it would probably have assumed an upright position. A white pine of about the same height lost its central shaft by a grub that developed from the egg of an insect, and I cut it away. It rose from a whorl of four branches, and it now devolved upon one of these to take the lead. Two of them, on opposite sides, were more vigorous than the other two, and the struggle now is as to which of these two shall gain the mastery. Both are rising up and turning toward the vacant chieftainship, and, unless something interferes, the tree will probably become forked and led upward by two equal branches. I shall probably humble the pride of one of the rivals by nipping its central shoot. One of my neighbors has cut off a yellow pine about six inches in diameter, so as to leave only one circle of limbs seven or eight feet from the ground. It is now the third year of the tree's decapitation, and one of this circle of horizontal limbs has risen up several feet, like a sleeper rising from his couch, and seems to be looking around inquiringly, as much as to say: "Come, brothers, wake up! Some one must take the lead here; shall it be I?"

In one of my Norway spruces I have witnessed the humbling or reducing to the ranks of a would-be

leading central shoot. For a couple of years the
vigorous young tree was led upward by two rival
branches; they appeared almost evenly matched;
but on the third year one of them clearly took the
lead, and at the end of the season was a foot or
more in advance of the other. The next year the
distance between them became still greater, and the
defeated leader appeared to give up the contest, so
that a season or two afterward it began to lose its
upright attitude and to fall more and more toward
a horizontal position; it was willing to go back into
the ranks of the lateral branches. Its humiliation
was so great that it even for a time dropped below
them; but toward midsummer it lifted up its head
a little, and was soon fairly in the position of a side
branch, simulating defeat and willing subordination
as completely as if it had been a conscious, sentient
being.

The evergreens can keep a secret the year round,
some one has said. How well they keep the secret
of the shedding of their leaves! so well that in the
case of the spruces we hardly know when it does
occur. In fact, the spruces do not properly shed
their leaves at all, but simply outgrow them, after
carrying them an indefinite time. Some of the species carry their leaves five or six years. The hemlock drops its leaves very irregularly: the winds
and the storms whip them off; in winter the snow
beneath them is often covered with them.

But the pine sheds its leaves periodically, though
always as it were stealthily and under cover of the

newer foliage. The white pine usually sheds its
leaves in midsummer, though I have known all the
pines to delay till October. It is on with the new
love before it is off with the old. From May till
near autumn it carries two crops of leaves, last
year's and the present year's. Emerson's inquiry,

> "How the sacred pine-tree adds
> To her old leaves new myriads,"

is framed in strict accordance with the facts. It is
to her *old* leaves that she adds the new. Only the
new growth, the outermost leaves, are carried over
till the next season, thus keeping the tree always
clothed and green. As its moulting season ap-
proaches, these old leaves, all the rear ranks on the
limbs, begin to turn yellow, and a careless observer
might think the tree was struck with death, but it
is not. The decay stops just where the growth of
the previous spring began, and presently the tree
stands green and vigorous, with a newly-laid carpet
of fallen leaves beneath it.

I wonder why it is that the pine has an ancient
look, a suggestion in some way of antiquity? Is
it because we know it to be the oldest tree? or is
it not rather that its repose, its silence, its un-
changeableness, suggest the past, and cause it to
stand out in sharp contrast upon the background
of the flitting, fugitive present? It has such a look
of permanence! When growing from the rocks, it
seems expressive of the same geologic antiquity as
they. It has the simplicity of primitive things;
the deciduous trees seem more complex, more het-

erogeneous; they have greater versatility, more resources. The pine has but one idea, and that is to
mount heavenward by regular steps, — tree. of fate,
tree of dark shadows and of mystery.

The pine is the tree of silence. Who was the
Goddess of Silence ! Look for her altars amid the
pines, — silence above, silence below. Pass from
deciduous woods into pine woods of a windy day,
and you think the day has suddenly become calm.
Then how silent to the foot! One walks over a
carpet of pine needles almost as noiselessly as over
the carpets of our dwellings. Do these halls lead
to the chambers of the great, that all noise should
be banished from them ! Let the designers come
here and get the true pattern for a carpet, — a soft
yellowish brown with only a red leaf, or a bit of
gray moss, or a dusky lichen scattered here and
there; a background that does not weary or bewil-
der the eye, or insult the ground-loving foot.

How friendly the pine-tree is to man, — so do-
cile and available as timber, and so warm and protective as shelter! Its balsam is salve to his wounds,
its fragrance is long life to his nostrils; an abiding,
perennial tree, tempering the climate, cool as mur-
muring waters in summer and like a wrapping of
fur in winter.

The deciduous trees are inconstant friends that
fail us when adverse winds do blow; but the pine
and all its tribe look winter cheerily in the face,
tossing the snow, masquerading in his arctic livery,
in fact holding high carnival from fall to spring.

The Norseman of the woods, lofty and aspiring, tree without bluster or noise, that sifts the howling storm into a fine spray of sound; symmetrical tree, tapering, columnar, shaped as in a lathe, the preordained mast of ships, the mother of colossal timbers; centralized, towering, patriarchal, coming down from the foreworld, counting centuries in thy rings and outlasting empires in thy decay.

A little tall talk seems not amiss on such a subject. The American or white pine has been known to grow to a height of two hundred and sixty feet, slender and tapering as a rush, and equally available for friction matches or the mast of a ship of the line. It is potent upon the sea and upon the land, and lends itself to become a standard for giants or a toy for babes, with equal readiness. No other tree so widely useful in the mechanic arts, or so beneficent in the economy of nature. House of refuge for the winter birds, and inn and hostelry for the spring and fall emigrants. All the northern creatures are more or less dependent upon the pine. Nature has made a singular exception in the conformation of the beaks of certain birds, that they might the better feed upon the seeds of its cones, as in the crossbills. Then the pine grosbeak and pine linnet are both nurslings of this tree. Certain of the warblers, also, the naturalist seldom finds except amid its branches.

The dominant races come from the region of the pine.

"Who liveth by the ragged pine
Foundeth a heroic line;"

says Emerson.

"Who liveth in the palace hall
Waneth fast and spendeth all."

The pines of Norway and Sweden sent out the
vikings, and out of the pine woods of northern
Europe came the virile barbarian overrunning the
effete southern countries.

"And grant to dwellers with the pine
Dominion o'er the palm and vine."

There is something sweet and piny about the northern literatures as contrasted with those of the voluble and passionate south, — something in them that
heals the mind's hurts like a finer balsam. In
reading Björnson, or Andersen, or Russian Turgé-
neff, though one may not be in contact with the
master spirits of the world, he is yet inhaling an
atmosphere that is resinous and curative; he is
under an influence that is arboreal, temperate, bal-
samic.

"The white pine," says Wilson Flagg in his
"Woods and By-Ways of New England," "has no
legendary history. Being an American tree, it is
celebrated neither in poetry nor romance." Not
perhaps in Old World poetry and romance, but certainly in that of the New World. The New England poets have not overlooked the pine, however
much they may have gone abroad for their themes
and tropes. Whittier's "My Playmate" is written
to the low monotone of the pine.

> "The pines were dark on Ramoth hill,
> Their song was soft and low;
> The blossoms in the sweet May wind
> Were falling like the snow."

Lowell's "To a Pine-Tree" is well known, —

> "Far up on Katahdin thou towerest
> Purple-blue with the distance and vast ;
> Like a cloud o'er the lowlands thou lowerest,
> That hangs poised on a lull in the blast
> To its fall leaning awful."

In his "A Mood" his attention is absorbed by this tree, and in the poet's quest of the muse he says, —

> "I haunt the pine-dark solitudes,
> With soft brown silence carpeted."

But the real white pine among our poets is Emerson. Against that rustling deciduous background of the New England poets he shows dark and aspiring. Emerson seems to have a closer fellowship with the pine than with any other tree, and it recurs again and again in his poems. In his "Garden" the pine is the principal vegetable, — "the snow-loving pines," as he so aptly says, and "the hemlocks tall, untamable." It is perhaps from the pine that he gets the idea that "Nature loves the number five;" its leaves are in fives and its whorl of branches is composed of five. His warbler is the "pine warbler," and he sees "the pigeons in the pines," where they are seldom to be seen. He even puts a "pine state-house" in his "Boston Hymn."

But, more than that, his "Woodnotes," one of his longest poems, is mainly the notes of the pine.

Theodore Parker said that a tree that talked like
Emerson's pine ought to be cut down; but if the
pine were to find a tongue, I should sooner expect
to hear the Emersonian dialect from it than almost
any other. It would be pretty high up, certainly,
and go over the heads of most of the other trees.
It were sure to be pointed, though the point few
could see. And it would not be garrulous and loud-
mouthed, though it might talk on and on. Whether
it would preach or not is a question, but I have no
doubt it would be a fragrant healing gospel if it
did. I think its sentences would be short ones
with long pauses between them, and that they
would sprout out of the subject independently and
not connect or interlock very much. There would
be breaks and chasms or maybe some darkness between the lines, but I should expect from it a lofty,
cheerful, and all-the-year-round philosophy. The
temptation to be oracular would no doubt be great,
and could be more readily overlooked in this tree
than in any other. Then, the pine being the oldest
tree, great wisdom and penetration might be expected of it.

Though Emerson's pine boasts

> " My garden is the cloven rock,
>   And my manure the snow;
>   And drifting sand-heaps feed my stock,
>   In summer's scorching glow," —

yet the great white pine loves a strong deep soil.
How it throve along our river bottom and pointed
out the best land to the early settlers! Remnants

of its stumps are still occasionally seen in land that
has been given to the plow these seventy or eighty
years.   In Pennsylvania the stumps are wrenched
from the ground by machinery and used largely for
fencing.   Laid upon their side with their wide
branching roots in the air, they form a barrier
before which even the hound-pursued deer may well
pause.

This aboriginal tree is fast disappearing from the
country. ˙ Its second growth seems to be a degen-
erate race, what the carpenters contemptuously call
pumpkin pine, on account of its softness.   All the
large tracts and provinces of the original tree have
been invaded and ravished by the lumbermen, so
that only isolated bands, and straggling specimens,
like the remnants of a defeated and disorganized
army, are now found scattered up and down the
country.   The spring floods on our northern rivers
have for decades of years been moving seething
walls of pine logs, sweeping down out of the wilderness.   I remember pausing beside a mammoth
pine in the Adirondack woods, standing a little to
one side of the destroyer's track, that must have
carried its green crown near one hundred and fifty
feet above the earth.   How such a tree impresses
one!   How it swells at the base and grows rigid as
if with muscular effort in its determined gripe of
the earth!   How it lays hold of the rocks, or rends
them asunder to secure its hold!   Nearly all trunk,
it seems to have shed its limbs like youthful follies
as it went skyward, or as the builders pull down

their scaffoldings and carry them higher as the tem-
ple mounts; nothing superfluous, no waste of time
or energy, the one purpose to cleave the empyrean
steadily held to.

At the Centennial fair I saw a section of a pine
from Canada that was eight feet in diameter, and
that had been growing, I have forgotten how many
centuries.   But this was only a sapling beside the
redwoods of California, one of which would carry
several such trees in his belt.

In the absence of the pine, the hemlock is a
graceful and noble tree.   In primitive woods it
shoots up in the same manner, drawing the ladder
up after it, and attains an altitude of nearly or
quite a hundred feet.   It is the poor man's pine,
and destined to humbler uses than its lordlier
brother.   It follows the pine like a servitor, keeping on higher and more rocky ground, and going
up the minor branch valleys when the pine follows
only the main or mother stream.   As an ornamental
tree it is very pleasing, and deserves to be cultivated
more than it is.   It is a great favorite with the
sylvan folk, too.   The ruffed grouse prefer it to
the pine; it is better shelter in winter, and its
buds are edible.   The red squirrel has found out
the seeds in its cones, and they are an important
part of his winter stores.   Some of the rarer warblers, too, like the Blackburnian and the blue yellow-back, I never find except among the hemlocks.
The older ornithologists, Audubon and Wilson,
named a "hemlock warbler" also, but this bird

turns out to be none other than the young of the Blackburnian described as a new species and named for its favorite tree.

All trees in primitive woods are less social, less disposed to intermingle, than trees in groves or fields: they are more heady; they meet only on high grounds; they shake hands over the heads of their neighbors; the struggle for life is sharper and more merciless, — in these and other respects suggesting men in cities. One tree falls against a more stanch one, and bruises only itself; a weaker one it carries to the ground with it.

Both the pine and the hemlock make friends with the birch, the maple, and the oak, and one of the most pleasing and striking features of our autumnal scenery is a mountain side sown broadcast with these intermingled trees, forming a combination of colors like the richest tapestry, the dark green giving body and permanence, the orange and yellow giving light and brilliancy.

III

HARD FARE

SUCH a winter as was that of 1880-81 — deep snows and zero weather for nearly three months — proves especially trying to the wild creatures that attempt to face it. The supply of fat (or fuel) with which their bodies become stored in the fall is rapidly exhausted by the severe and uninterrupted cold, and the sources from which fresh supplies are usually obtained are all but wiped out. Even the fox was very hard pressed and reduced to the unusual straits of eating frozen apples; the pressure of hunger must be great, indeed, to compel Reynard to take up with such a diet. A dog will eat corn, but he cannot digest it, and I doubt if the fox extracted anything more than the cider from the frozen and thawed apples. They perhaps served to amuse and occupy his stomach for the time. Humboldt says wolves eat earth, especially clay, during winter, and Pliny makes a similar observation. In Greenland the dog eats seaweed when other food fails. In tropical countries, during the tropical winter, many savage tribes eat clay. It distends their stomachs, and in a measure satisfies the cravings of hunger. During the season referred to, the

crows appeared to have little else than frozen apples
for many weeks; they hung about the orchards as
a last resort, and, after scouring the desolate landscape over, would return to their cider with resig-
nation, but not with cheerful alacrity.   They grew
very bold at times, and ventured quite under my
porch, and filched the bones that Lark, the dog,
had left.   I put out some corn on the wall near by,
and discovered that crows will not eat corn in the
winter, except as they can break up the kernels.
It is too hard for their gizzards to grind.   Then
the crow, not being properly a granivorous bird,
but a carnivorous, has not the digestive, or rather
the pulverizing power of the domestic fowls.   The
difficulty also during such a season of coming at the
soil and obtaining gravel-stones, which, in such
cases, are really the millstones, may also have
something to do with it.   Corn that has been
planted and has sprouted, crows will swallow readily enough, because it is then soft, and is easily
ground.   My impression has always been that in
spring and summer they will also pick up any
chance kernels the planters may have dropped.   But,
as I observed them the past winter, they always
held the kernel under one foot upon the wall, and
picked it to pieces before devouring it.   This is the
manner of the jays also.   The jays, perhaps, had a
tougher time during the winter than the crows,
because they do not eat fish or flesh, but depend
mainly upon nuts.   A troop of them came eagerly
to my ash-heap one morning, which had just been

uncovered by the thaw, but they found little except
cinders for their gizzards, which, maybe, was what
they wanted. They had foraged nearly all winter
upon my neighbor's corn-crib, and probably their
millstones were dull and needed replacing. They
reached the corn through the opening between the
slats, and were the envy of the crows, who watched
them from the near trees, but dared not venture
up. The chickadee, which is an insectivorous bird,
will eat corn in winter. It will carry a kernel to
the limb of a tree, where, held beneath its tiny
foot, it will peck out the eye or chit of the corn, —
the germinal part only. I have also seen the woodpecker in winter eat the berries of the poison ivy.
Quails will eat the fruit of the poison sumac, and
grouse are killed with their crops distended with
the leaves of the laurel. Grouse also eat the berries of the bitter-sweet.

The general belief among country-people that the
jay hoards up nuts for winter use has probably
some foundation in fact, though one is at a loss to
know where he could place his stores so that they
would not be pilfered by the mice and the squirrels.
An old hunter told me he had seen jays secreting
beechnuts in a knothole in a tree. Probably a
red squirrel saw them, too, and laughed behind his
tail. One day, in October, two friends of mine,
out hunting, saw a blue jay carrying off chestnuts
to a spruce swamp. He came and went with great
secrecy and dispatch. He had several hundred
yards to fly each way, but occupied only a few

minutes each trip. The hunters lay in wait to shoot him, but so quickly would he seize his chestnut and be off, that he made more than a dozen trips before they killed him.

A lady writing to me from Iowa says: "I must tell you what I saw a blue jay do last winter. Flying down to the ground in front of the house, he put something in the dead grass, drawing the grass over it, first on one side, then on the other, tramped it down just exactly as a squirrel would, then walked around the spot, examining it to see if it was satisfactory. After he had flown away, I went out to see what he had hidden; it was a nicely shucked peanut that he had laid up for a time of scarcity." Since then I have myself made similar observations. I have several times seen jays carry off chestnuts and hide them here and there upon the ground. They put only one in a place, and covered it up with grass or leaves. Instead, therefore, of hoarding up nuts for future use, when the jay carries them off, he is really planting them. When the snows come these nuts are lost to him, even if he remembered the hundreds of places where he had dropped them. May not this fact account in a measure for the oak and chestnut trees that spring up where a pine forest has been cleared from the ground? Probably the crows secrete nuts in the same way. The acorns at least germinate and remain small, insignificant shoots until the pine is cut away and they have a chance. In almost any pine wood these baby oaks may be seen scattered

here and there. Jays will carry off and secrete corn
in the same way. One winter I put out ears of
corn near my study window to attract these birds.
They were not long in finding them out, nor long
in stripping the cob of its kernels. They finally
came to the window-sill and picked up the loose
kernels I scattered there. At no time did they eat
any on the spot, but were solely intent on carrying
it away. They would take eight or ten grains at
a time, apparently holding it in the throat and bill.
They carried it away and deposited it in all manner
of places; sometimes on the ground, sometimes in
decayed trees. Once I saw a jay deposit his load
in an old worm's nest in a near-by apple-tree.
Whether these stores were visited afterward by the
birds, I cannot say. Red-headed woodpeckers have
been seen to fill crevices in posts and rails with
acorns, where they were found and eaten by gray
squirrels. Oregon and Mexican woodpeckers drill
holes in decayed trees, and store them with acorns,
putting but one acorn in a hole, but hundreds of
holes in a tree or branch.

A bevy of quail in my vicinity got through the
winter by feeding upon the little black beans contained in the pods of the common locust. For many
weeks their diet must have been almost entirely
leguminous. The surface snow in the locust-grove
which they frequented was crossed in every direction with their fine tracks, like a chain-stitch upon
muslins, showing where they went from pod to pod
and extracted the contents. Where quite a large

branch, filled with pods, lay upon the snow, it looked as if the whole flock had dined or breakfasted off it. The wind seemed to shake down the pods about as fast as they were needed. When a fresh fall of snow had blotted out everything, it was not many hours before the wind had placed upon the cloth another course; but it was always the same old course — beans, beans. What would the birds and the fowls do during such winters, if the trees and the shrubs and plants all dropped their fruit and their seeds in the fall, as they do their leaves? They would nearly all perish. The apples that cling to the trees, the pods that hang to the lowest branches, and the seeds that the various weeds and grasses hold above the deepest snows, alone make it possible for many birds to pass the winter among us. The red squirrel, too, what would he do? He lays up no stores like the provident chipmunk, but scours about for food in all weathers, feeding upon the seeds in the cones of the hemlock that still cling to the tree, upon sumac-bobs, and the seeds of frozen apples. I have seen the ground under a wild apple-tree that stood near the woods completely covered with the "chonkings" of the frozen apples, the work of the squirrels in getting at the seeds; not an apple had been left, and apparently not a seed had been lost. But the squirrels in this particular locality evidently got pretty hard up before spring, for they developed a new source of food-supply. A young bushy-topped sugar-ma-
bout forty feet high, standing beside a stone

fence near the woods, was attacked, and more than half denuded of its bark. The object of the squirrels seemed to be to get at the soft, white, mucilaginous substance (cambium layer) between the bark and the wood. The ground was covered with fragments of the bark, and the white, naked stems and branches had been scraped by fine teeth. When the sap starts in the early spring, the squirrels add this to their scanty supplies. They perforate the bark of the branches of the maples with their chisel-like teeth, and suck the sweet liquid as it slowly oozes out. It is not much as food, but evidently it helps.

I have said the red squirrel does not lay by a store of food for winter use, like the chipmunk and the wood-mice; yet in the fall he sometimes hoards in a tentative, temporary kind of way. I have seen his savings — butternuts and black walnuts — stuck here and there in saplings and trees near his nest; sometimes carefully inserted in the upright fork of a limb or twig. One day, late in November, I counted a dozen or more black walnuts put away in this manner in a little grove of locusts, chestnuts, and maples by the roadside, and could but smile at the wise forethought of the rascally squirrel. His supplies were probably safer that way than if more elaborately hidden. They were well distributed; his eggs were not all in one basket, and he could go away from home without any fear that his storehouse would be broken into in his absence. The next week, when I passed that way, the nuts were all gone but two. I saw the squirrel that doubtless laid claim to them, on each occasion.

There is one thing the red squirrel knows unerringly that I do not (there are probably several other things); that is, on which side of the butternut the meat lies. He always gnaws through the shell so as to strike the kernel broadside, and thus easily extract it; while to my eyes there is no external mark or indication, in the form or appearance of the nut, as there is in the hickory-nut, by which I can tell whether the edge or the side of the meat is toward me. But examine any number of nuts that the squirrels have rifled, and, as a rule, you will find they always drill through the shell at the one spot where the meat will be most exposed. It stands them in hand to know, and they do know. Doubtless, if butternuts were a main source of my food, and I were compelled to gnaw into them, I should learn, too, on which side my bread was buttered.

A hard winter affects the chipmunks very little; they are snug and warm in their burrows in the ground and under the rocks, with a bountiful store of nuts or grain. I have heard of nearly a half-bushel of chestnuts being taken from a single den. They usually hole in November, and do not come out again till March or April, unless the winter is very open and mild. Gray squirrels, when they have been partly domesticated in parks and groves near dwellings, are said to hide their nuts here and there upon the ground, and in winter to dig them

up from beneath the snow, always hitting the spot
accurately. A pair of flying squirrels which I observed one season in an unoccupied country-house
had a pile of large, fine chestnuts near their nest
till spring, when the nuts disappeared. They probably kept them till the period of greatest scarcity,
and until their young made demands upon them.

The woodpeckers and chickadees doubtless find
food as plentiful during severe winters as during
more open ones, because they confine their search
almost entirely to the trunks and branches of trees,
where the latter pick up the eggs of insects and
various microscopic tidbits, and where the former
find their accustomed fare of eggs and larvæ also.
An enamel of ice upon the trees alone puts an
embargo upon their supplies. At such seasons the
ruffed grouse "buds" or goes hungry; while the
snowbirds, snow buntings, Canada sparrows, goldfinches, shore larks, and redpolls are dependent
upon the weeds and grasses that rise above the
snow, and upon the litter of the haystack and barn-
yard. Neither do the deep snows and the severe
cold materially affect the supplies of the rabbit.
The deeper the snow, the nearer he is brought to
the tops of the tender bushes and shoots. I see in
my walks where he has cropped the tops of the
small, bushy, soft maples, cutting them slantingly
as you would do with a knife, and quite as smoothly.
Indeed, the mark was so like that of a knife that,
notwithstanding the tracks, it was only after the
closest scrutiny that I was convinced it was the

sharp, chisel-like teeth of the rabbit. He leaves no chips, and apparently makes clean work of every twig he cuts off.

The wild or native mice usually lay up stores in the fall, in the shape of various nuts, grain, and seeds, yet the provident instinct, as in the red squirrel and in the jay, seems only partly developed in them; instead of carrying these supplies home, they hide them in the nearest convenient place. I have known them to carry a pint or more of hickory nuts and deposit them in a pair of boots standing in the chamber of an outhouse. Near the chestnut-trees they will fill little pocket-like depressions in the ground with chestnuts; in a grain-field they carry the grain under stones; under some cover beneath cherry-trees they collect great numbers of cherry-pits. Hence, when cold weather comes, instead of staying at home like the chipmunk, they gad about hither and thither looking up their supplies. One may see their tracks on the snow everywhere in the woods and fields and by the roadside. The advantage of this way of living is that it leads to activity, and probably to sociability.

These wild mice are fond of bees and of honey, and they apparently like nothing better than to be allowed to take up their quarters in winter in some vacant space in a hive of bees. A chamber just over the bees seems to be preferred, as here they get the benefit of the warmth generated by the insects. One very cold winter I wrapped up one

of my hives with my shawl. Before long I noticed
that the shawl was beginning to have a very torn
and tattered appearance. On examination, I found
that a native mouse had established itself in the
top of the hive, and had levied a ruinous tax upon
the shawl to make itself a nest. Never was a
fabric more completely reduced into its original elements than were large sections of that shawl. It
was a masterly piece of analysis. The work of the
wheel and the loom was exactly reversed, and what
was once shawl was now the finest and softest of
wool. The white-footed mouse is much more common along the fences and in the woods than one
would suspect. One winter day I set a mouse-trap
— the kind known as the delusion trap — beneath
some ledges in the edge of the woods, to determine
what species of mouse was most active at this season. The snow fell so deeply that I did not visit
my trap for two or three weeks. When I did so,
it was literally packed full of white-footed mice.
There were seven in all, and not room for another.
Our woods are full of these little creatures, and
they appear to have a happy, social time of it, even
in the severest winters. Their little tunnels under
the snow and their hurried strides upon its surface
may be noted everywhere. They link tree and
stump, or rock and tree, by their pretty trails.
They evidently travel for adventure and to hear the
news, as well as for food. They know that foxes
and owls are about, and they keep pretty close to
cover. When they cross an exposed place, they do
it hurriedly.

Such a winter as I have referred to probably
destroys a great many of our half-migratory birds.
The mortality appears to be the greatest in the
Border States, where so many species, like the
sparrows, robins, bluebirds, meadowlarks, kinglets,
etc., usually pass the cold season. A great many
birds are said to have died in New Jersey and
Pennsylvania, including game-birds. A man in
Chester County saw a fox digging in the snow; on
examining the spot, he found half a dozen quails
frozen to death. Game-birds and nearly all other
birds will stand the severest weather if food is
plenty; but to hunger and cold both, the hardiest
species may succumb.

Meadowlarks often pass the winter as far north
as Pennsylvania. A man residing in that State
relates how, in the height of the severest cold, three
half-famished larks came to his door in quest of
food. He removed the snow from a small space,
and spread the poor birds a lunch of various grains
and seeds. They ate heartily, and returned again
the next day, and the next, each time bringing one
or more drooping and half-starved companions with
them, till there was quite a flock of them. Their
deportment changed, their forms became erect and
their plumage glossy, and the feeble mendicants became strong and vivacious birds again. These larks
fell in good hands, but I am persuaded that this
species suffered more than any other of our birds
during that winter. In the spring they were unusually late in making their appearance, — the first one

noted by me on the 9th of April, — and they were scarce in my locality during the whole season.

Birds not of a feather flock together in winter. Hard times or a common misfortune makes all the world akin. A Noah's ark with antagonistic species living in harmony is not an improbable circumstance in a forty-day and a forty-night rain. In severe weather, when the snow lies deep on the ground, I frequently see a loose, heterogeneous troop of birds pass my door, engaged in the common search for food: snowbirds, Canada sparrows, and goldfinches on the ground, and kinglets and nuthatches in the tree above, — all drifting slowly in the same direction, — the snowbirds and sparrows closely associated, but the goldfinches rather clannish and exclusive, while the kinglets and nuthatches keep still more aloof. These birds were probably not drawn, even thus loosely, together by any social instincts, but by a common want; all were hungry, and the activity of one species attracted and drew after it another and another. "I will look that way, too," the kinglet and creeper probably said, when they saw the other birds busy, and heard their merry voices.

•

IV

THE TRAGEDIES OF THE NESTS

THE life of the birds, especially of our migratory
song-birds, is a series of adventures and of hair-
breadth escapes by flood and field. Very few of
them probably die a natural death, or even live out
half their appointed days. The home instinct is
strong in birds, as it is in most creatures; and I
am convinced that every spring a large number of
those which have survived the Southern campaign
return to their old haunts to breed. A Connecticut
farmer took me out under his porch one April day,
and showed me a phœbe-bird's nest six stories high.
The same bird had no doubt returned year after
year; and as there was room for only one nest upon
her favorite shelf, she had each season reared a new
superstructure upon the old as a foundation. I
have heard of a white robin — an albino — that
nested several years in succession in the suburbs of
a Maryland city. A sparrow with a very marked
peculiarity of song I have heard several seasons
in my own locality. But the birds do not all live
to return to their old haunts: the bobolinks and
starlings run a gauntlet of fire from the Hudson to
the Savannah, and the robins and meadowlarks and

other song-birds are shot by boys and pot-hunters
in great numbers, —to say nothing of their danger
from hawks and owls. But of those that do return,
what perils beset their nests, even in the most
favored localities! The cabins of the early settlers,
when the country was swarming with hostile Indians, were not surrounded by such dangers. The
tender households of the birds are not only exposed
to hostile Indians in the shape of cats and collectors, but to numerous murderous and bloodthirsty
animals, against whom they have no defense but
concealment. They lead the darkest kind of pioneer
life, even in our gardens and orchards, and under
the walls of our houses. Not a day or a night
passes, from the time the eggs are laid till the
young are flown, when the chances are not greatly
in favor of the nest being rifled and its contents
devoured, — by owls, skunks, minks, and coons at
night, and by crows, jays, squirrels, weasels,
snakes, and rats during the day. Infancy, we say,
is hedged about by many perils; but the infancy of
birds is cradled and pillowed in peril. An old
Michigan settler told me that the first six children
that were born to him died; malaria and teething
invariably carried them off when they had reached
a certain age; but other children were born, the
country improved, and by and by the babies weath-
ered the critical period, and the next six lived
and grew up. The birds, too, would no doubt
persevere six times and twice six times, if the season were long enough, and finally rear their family,

but the waning summer cuts them short, and but
few species have the heart and strength to make
even the third trial.

The first nest-builders in spring, like the first
settlers near hostile tribes, suffer the most casual-
ties.   A large proportion of the nests of April and
May are destroyed; their enemies have been many
months without eggs, and their appetites are keen
for them.   It is a time, too, when other food is
scarce, and the crows and squirrels are hard put.
But the second nests of June, and still more the
nests of July and August, are seldom molested.
It is rarely that the nest of the goldfinch or cedar-
bird is harried.

My neighborhood on the Hudson is perhaps exceptionally unfavorable as a breeding haunt for birds,
owing to the abundance of fish crows and of red
squirrels; and the season of which this chapter is
mainly a chronicle, the season of 1881, seems to
have been a black-letter one even for this place, for
at least nine nests out of every ten that I observed
during that spring and summer failed of their
proper issue.   From the first nest I noted, which
was that of a bluebird, — built (very imprudently,
I thought at the time) in a squirrel-hole in a
decayed apple-tree, about the last of April, and
which came to naught, even the mother-bird, I
suspect, perishing by a violent death, — to the last,
which was that of a snowbird, observed in August,
among the Catskills, deftly concealed in a mossy
bank by the side of a road that skirted a wood,

where the tall thimble blackberries grew in abundance, and from which the last young one was taken, when it was about half grown, by some nocturnal walker or daylight prowler, some untoward fate seemed hovering about them. It was a season of calamities, of violent deaths, of pillage and massacre, among our feathered neighbors. For the first time I noticed that the orioles were not safe in their strong pendent nests. Three broods were started in the apple-trees, only a few yards from the house, where, for several previous seasons, the birds had nested without molestation; but this time the young were all destroyed when about half grown. Their chirping and chattering, which was so noticeable one day, suddenly ceased the next. The nests were probably plundered at night, and doubtless by the little red screech owl, which I know is a denizen of these old orchards, living in the deeper cavities of the trees. The owl could alight upon the top of the nest, and easily thrust his murderous claw down into its long pocket and seize the young and draw them forth. The tragedy of one of the nests was heightened, or at least made more palpable, by one of the half-fledged birds, either in its attempt to escape or while in the clutches of the enemy, being caught and entangled in one of the horse-hairs by which the nest was stayed and held to the limb above. There it hung bruised and dead, gibbeted to its own cradle. This nest was the theatre of another little tragedy later in the season. Some time in August a bluebird,

indulging its propensity to peep and pry into holes
and crevices, alighted upon it and probably in-
spected the interior; but by some unlucky move it
got its wings entangled in this same fatal horse-hair.
Its efforts to free itself appeared only to result in
its being more securely and hopelessly bound; and
there it perished; and there its form, dried and
embalmed by the summer heats, was yet hanging
in September, the outspread wings and plumage
showing nearly as bright as in life.

A correspondent writes me that one of his orioles
got entangled in a cord while building her nest,
and that, though by the aid of a ladder he reached
and liberated her, she died soon afterward.   He
also found a "chippie" (called also "hair-bird")
suspended from a branch by a horse-hair, beneath
a partly-constructed nest.   I heard of a cedar-bird
caught and destroyed in the same way, and of two
young bluebirds, around whose legs a horse-hair
had become so tightly wound that the legs withered
up and dropped off.   The birds became fledged,
and finally left the nest with the others.   Such
tragedies are probably quite common.

Before the advent of civilization in this country,
the oriole probably built a much deeper nest than
it usually does at present.   When now it builds in
remote trees and along the borders of the woods,
its nest, I have noticed, is long and gourd-shaped;
but in orchards and near dwellings it is only a deep
cup or pouch.   It shortens it up in proportion as
the danger lessens.   Probably a succession of disas-

trous years, like the one under review, would cause
it to lengthen it again beyond the reach of owl's
talons or jay-bird's beak.

The first song sparrow's nest I observed in the
spring of 1881 was in a field under a fragment of
a board, the board being raised from the ground a
couple of inches by two poles.   It had its full com-
plement of eggs, and probably sent forth a brood of
young birds, though as to this I cannot speak positively, as I neglected to observe it further.   It was
well sheltered and concealed, and was not easily
come at by any of its natural enemies, save snakes
and weasels.   But concealment often avails little.
In May, a song sparrow, which had evidently met
with disaster earlier in the season, built its nest in
a thick mass of woodbine against the side of my
house, about fifteen feet from the ground.   Perhaps
it took the hint from its cousin, the English sparrow.   The nest was admirably placed, protected
from the storms by the overhanging eaves and from
all eyes by the thick screen of leaves.   Only by
patiently watching the suspicious bird, as she lingered near with food in her beak, did I discover
its whereabouts.   That brood is safe, I thought,
beyond doubt.   But it was not: the nest was pil-
laged one night, either by an owl, or else by a rat
that had climbed into the vine, seeking an entrance
to the house.   The mother bird, after reflecting
upon her ill-luck about a week, seemed to resolve
to try a different system of tactics, and to throw all
appearances of concealment aside.   She built a nest

a few yards from the house, beside the drive, upon
a smooth piece of greensward. There was not a
weed or a shrub or anything whatever to conceal it
or mark its site. The structure was completed,
and incubation had begun, before I discovered what
was going on. "Well, well," I said, looking down
upon the bird almost at my feet, "this is going to
the other extreme indeed; now the cats will have
you." The desperate little bird sat there day after
day, looking like a brown leaf pressed down in the
short green grass. As the weather grew hot, her
position became very trying. It was no longer a
question of keeping the eggs warm, but of keeping
them from roasting. The sun had no mercy on
her, and she fairly panted in the middle of the
day. In such an emergency the male robin has
been known to perch above the sitting female and
shade her with his outstretched wings. But in this
case there was no perch for the male bird, had he
been disposed to make a sunshade of himself. I
thought to lend a hand in this direction myself,
and so stuck a leafy twig beside the nest. This
was probably an unwise interference: it guided
disaster to the spot; the nest was broken up, and
the mother bird was probably caught, as I never
saw her afterward.

For several previous summers a pair of kingbirds
had reared, unmolested, a brood of young in an
apple-tree, only a few yards from the house; but
during this season disaster overtook them also.
The nest was completed, the eggs laid, and incuba-

tion had just begun, when, one morning about sunrise, I heard loud cries of distress and alarm proceed from the old apple-tree.   Looking out of the
window, I saw a crow, which I knew to be a fish
crow, perched upon the edge of the nest, hastily
bolting the eggs.   The parent birds, usually so
ready for the attack, seemed overcome with grief
and alarm.   They fluttered about in the most helpless and bewildered manner, and it was not till the
robber fled on my approach that they recovered
themselves and charged upon him.   The crow scur-
ried away with upturned, threatening head, the
furious kingbirds fairly upon his back.   The pair
lingered around their desecrated nest for several
days, almost silent, and saddened by their loss, and
then disappeared.   They probably made another
trial elsewhere.

The fish crow only fishes when it has destroyed
all the eggs and young birds it can find.   It is the
most despicable thief and robber among our feathered creatures.   From May to August it is gorged
with the fledgelings of the nest.   It is fortunate
that its range is so limited.   In size it is smaller
than the common crow, and is a much less noble
and dignified bird.   Its caw is weak and feminine,
—a sort of split and abortive caw, that stamps it
the sneak-thief it is.   This crow is common farther
south, but is not found in this State, so far as I
have observed, except in the valley of the Hudson.

One season a pair of them built a nest in a Norway spruce that stood amid a dense growth of other

ornamental trees near a large unoccupied house.
They sat down amid plenty.   The wolf established
himself in the fold.   The many birds — robins,
thrushes, finches, vireos, pewees — that seek the
vicinity of dwellings (especially of these large country residences with their many trees and park-like
grounds), for the greater safety of their eggs and
young, were the easy and convenient victims of
these robbers.   They plundered right and left, and
were not disturbed till their young were nearly
fledged, when some boys, who had long before
marked them as their prize, rifled the nest.

The song-birds nearly all build low; their cradle
is not upon the treetop.   It is only birds of prey
that fear danger from below more than from above,
and that seek the higher branches for their nests.
A line five feet from the ground would run above
more than half the nests, and one ten feet would
bound more than three fourths of them.   It is only
the oriole, the wood pewee, the tanager, the war-
bling vireo, and two or three warblers, that, as a
rule, go higher than this.   The crows and jays and
other enemies of the birds have learned to explore
this belt pretty thoroughly.   But the leaves and
the protective coloring of most nests baffle them as
effectually, no doubt, as they do the professional
oologist.   The nest of the red-eyed vireo is one of
the most artfully placed in the wood.   It is just
beyond the point where the eye naturally pauses in
its search; namely, on the extreme end of the
lowest branch of the tree, usually four or five feet

from the ground. One looks up and down and through the tree, — shoots his eye-beams into it as he might discharge his gun at some game hidden there, but the drooping tip of that low horizontal branch, — who would think of pointing his piece just there? If a crow or other marauder were to alight upon the branch or upon those above it, the nest would be screened from him by the large leaf that usually forms a canopy immediately above it. The nest-hunter, standing at the foot of the tree and looking straight before him, might discover it easily, were it not for its soft, neutral gray tint which blends so thoroughly with the trunks and branches of trees. Indeed, I think there is no nest in the woods — no arboreal nest — so well concealed. The last one I saw was pendent from the end of a low branch of a maple, that nearly grazed the clapboards of an unused hay-barn in a remote backwoods clearing. I peeped through a crack, and saw the old birds feed the nearly fledged young within a few inches of my face. And yet the cowbird finds this nest and drops her parasitical egg in it. Her tactics in this as in other cases are probably to watch the movements of the parent bird. She may often be seen searching anxiously through the trees or bushes for a suitable nest, yet she may still oftener be seen perched upon some good point of observation watching the birds as they come and go about her. There is no doubt that, in many cases, the cowbird makes room for her own illegitimate egg in the nest by removing one of the bird's own.

When the cowbird finds two or more eggs in a
nest in which she wishes to deposit her own, she
will remove one of them. I found a sparrow's nest
with two sparrow's eggs and one cowbird's egg, and
another egg lying a foot or so below it on the
ground. I replaced the ejected egg, and the next
day found it again removed, and another cowbird's
egg in its place. I put it back the second time,
when it was again ejected, or destroyed, for I failed
to find it anywhere. Very alert and sensitive birds
like the warblers, often bury the strange egg beneath
a second nest built on top of the old. A lady,
living in the suburbs of an eastern city, one morning heard cries of distress from a pair of house
wrens that had a nest in a honeysuckle on her front
porch. On looking out of the window, she beheld
this little comedy, — comedy from her point of
view, but no doubt grim tragedy from the point of
view of the wrens: a cowbird with a wren's egg in
its beak running rapidly along the walk, with the
outraged wrens forming a procession behind it,
screaming, scolding, and gesticulating as only these
voluble little birds can. The cowbird had probably
been surprised in the act of violating the nest, and
the wrens were giving her a piece of their minds.

Every cowbird is reared at the expense of two or
more song-birds. For every one of these dusky
little pedestrians there amid the grazing cattle there
are two or more sparrows, or vireos, or warblers,
the less. It is a big price to pay, — two larks for
a bunting, — two sovereigns for a shilling; but

Nature does not hesitate occasionally to contradict herself in just this way. The young of the cowbird is disproportionately large and aggressive, one might say hoggish. When disturbed, it will clasp the nest and scream and snap its beak threateningly. One hatched out in a song sparrow's nest which was under my observation, and would soon have overridden and overborne the young sparrow which came out of the shell a few hours later, had I not interfered from time to time and lent the young sparrow a helping hand. Every day I would visit the nest and take the sparrow out from under the pot-bellied interloper, and place it on top, so that presently it was able to hold its own against its enemy. Both birds became fledged and left the nest about the same time. Whether the race was an even one after that, I know not.

I noted but two warblers' nests during that season, one of the black-throated blue-back and one of the redstart, — the latter built in an apple-tree but a few yards from a little rustic summer-house where I idle away many summer days. The lively little birds, darting and flashing about, attracted my attention for a week before I discovered their nest. They probably built it by working early in the morning, before I appeared upon the scene, as I never saw them with material in their beaks. Guessing from their movements that the nest was in a large maple that stood near by, I climbed the tree and explored it thoroughly, looking especially in the forks of the branches, as the authorities say

these birds build in a fork. But no nest could I
find. Indeed, how can one by searching find a
bird's nest? I overshot the mark; the nest was
much nearer me, almost under my very nose, and
I discovered it, not by searching, but by a casual
glance of the eye, while thinking of other matters.
The bird was just settling upon it as I looked up
from my book and caught her in the act. The nest
was built near the end of a long, knotty, horizontal
branch of an apple-tree, but effectually hidden by
the grouping of the leaves; it had three eggs, one
of which proved to be barren. The two young
birds grew apace, and were out of the nest early in
the second week; but something caught one of them
the first night. The other probably grew to maturity, as it disappeared from the vicinity with its
parents after some days.

The blue-back's nest was scarcely a foot from
the ground, in a little bush situated in a low,
dense wood of hemlock and beech and maple amid
the Catskills, — a deep, massive, elaborate structure, in which the sitting bird sank till her beak
and tail alone were visible above the brim. It was
a misty, chilly day when I chanced to find the
nest, and the mother bird knew instinctively that
it was not prudent to leave her four half-incubated
eggs uncovered and exposed for a moment. When
I sat down near the nest, she grew very uneasy,
and, after trying in vain to decoy me away by suddenly dropping from the branches and dragging
herself over the ground as if mortally wounded, she

approached and timidly and half doubtingly covered
her eggs within two yards of where I sat.   I disturbed her several times, to note her ways.   There
came to be something almost appealing in her looks
and manner, and she would keep her place on her
precious eggs till my outstretched hand was within
a few feet of her.   Finally, I covered the cavity of
the nest with a dry leaf.   This she did not remove
with her beak, but thrust her head deftly beneath
it and shook it off upon the ground.   Many of her
sympathizing neighbors, attracted by her alarm note,
came and had a peep at the intruder, and then flew
away, but the male bird did not appear upon the
scene.   The final history of this nest I am unable
to give, as I did not again visit it till late in the
season, when, of course, it was empty.

Years pass without my finding a brown thrasher's
nest; it is not a nest you are likely to stumble
upon in your walk; it is hidden as a miser hides
his gold, and watched as jealously.   The male pours
out his rich and triumphant song from the tallest
tree he can find, and fairly challenges you to come
and look for his treasures in his vicinity.   But you
will not find them if you go.   The nest is somewhere on the outer circle of his song; he is never
so imprudent as to take up his stand very near it.
The artists who draw those cozy little pictures of
a brooding mother bird, with the male perched but
a yard away in full song, do not copy from nature.
The thrasher's nest I found was thirty or forty rods
from the point where the male was wont to indulge

in his brilliant recitative. It was in an open field
under a low ground-juniper. My dog disturbed
the sitting bird as I was passing near. The nest
could be seen only by lifting up and parting away
the branches. All the arts of concealment had
been carefully studied. It was the last place you
would think of looking, and, if you did look,
nothing was visible but the dense green circle of
the low-spreading juniper. When you approached,
the bird would keep her place till you had begun
to stir the branches, when she would start out, and,
just skimming the ground, make a bright brown
line to the near fence and bushes. I confidently
expected that this nest would escape molestation,
but it did not. Its discovery by myself and dog
probably opened the door for ill-luck, as one day,
not long afterward, when I peeped in upon it, it
was empty. The proud song of the male had ceased
from his accustomed tree, and the pair were seen
no more in that vicinity.

The phœbe-bird is a wise architect, and perhaps
enjoys as great an immunity from danger, both in
its person and its nest, as any other bird. Its
modest, ashen-gray suit is the color of the rocks
where it builds, and the moss of which it makes
such free use gives to its nest the look of a natural
growth or accretion. But when it comes into the
barn or under the shed to build, as it so frequently
does, the moss is rather out of place. Doubtless
in time the bird will take the hint, and when she
builds in such places will leave the moss out. I

noted but two nests the summer I am speaking of:
one in a barn failed of issue, on account of the rats,
I suspect, though the little owl may have been the
depredator; the other, in the woods, sent forth
three young.　This latter nest was most charmingly
and ingeniously placed.　I discovered it while in
quest of pond-lilies, in a long, deep, level stretch
of water in the woods.　A large tree had blown
over at the edge of the water, and its dense mass of
upturned roots, with the black, peaty soil filling
the interstices, was like the fragment of a wall
several feet high, rising from the edge of the lan-
guid current.　In a niche in this earthy wall, and
visible and accessible only from the water, a phœbe
had built her nest and reared her brood.　I paddled
my boat up and came alongside prepared to take the
family aboard.　The young, nearly ready to fly,
were quite undisturbed by my presence, having
probably been assured that no danger need be appre-
hended from that side.　It was not a likely place
for minks, or they would not have been so secure.

I noted but one nest of the wood pewee, and
that, too, like so many other nests, failed of issue.
It was saddled upon a small dry limb of a plane-
tree that stood by the roadside, about forty feet
from the ground.　Every day for nearly a week, as
I passed by, I saw the sitting bird upon the nest.
Then one morning she was not in her place, and
on examination the nest proved to be empty, —
robbed, I had no doubt, by the red squirrels, as
they were very abundant in its vicinity, and ap-

peared to make a clean sweep of every nest. The
wood pewee builds an exquisite nest, shaped and
finished as if cast in a mould. It is modeled without and within with equal neatness and art, like
the nest of the hummingbird and the little gray
gnatcatcher. The material is much more refractory
than that used by either of these birds, being, in
the present case, dry, fine cedar twigs; but these
were bound into a shape as rounded and compact as
could be moulded out of the most plastic material.
Indeed, the nest of this bird looks precisely like
a large, lichen-covered, cup-shaped excrescence of
the limb upon which it is placed. And the bird,
while sitting, seems entirely at her ease. Most
birds seem to make very hard work of incubation.
It is a kind of martyrdom which appears to tax all
their powers of endurance. They have such a
fixed, rigid, predetermined look, pressed down into
the nest and as motionless as if made of cast-iron.
But the wood pewee is an exception. She is
largely visible above the rim of the nest. Her attitude is easy and graceful; she moves her head this
way and that, and seems to take note of whatever
goes on about her; and if her neighbor were to
drop in for a little social chat, she could doubtless
do her part. In fact, she makes light and easy
work of what, to most other birds, is such a serious
and engrossing matter. If it does not look like
play with her, it at least looks like leisure and
quiet contemplation.

There is no nest-builder that suffers more from

crows and squirrels and other enemies than the wood thrush. It builds as openly and unsuspiciously as if it thought all the world as honest as itself. Its favorite place is the fork of a sapling, eight or ten feet from the ground, where it falls an easy prey to every nest-robber that comes prowling through the woods and groves. It is not a bird that skulks and hides, like the catbird, the brown thrasher, the chat, or the chewink, and its nest is not concealed with the same art as theirs. Our thrushes are all frank, open-mannered birds; but the veery and the hermit build upon the ground, where they at least escape the crows, owls, and jays, and stand a better chance to be overlooked by the red squirrel and weasel also; while the robin seeks the protection of dwellings and outbuildings. For years I have not known the nest of a wood thrush to succeed. During the season referred to I observed but two, both apparently a second attempt, as the season was well advanced, and both failures. In one case, the nest was placed in a branch that an apple-tree, standing near a dwelling, held out over the highway. The structure was barely ten feet above the middle of the road, and would just escape a passing load of hay. It was made conspicuous by the use of a large fragment of newspaper in its foundation, — an unsafe material to build upon in most cases. Whatever else the press may guard, this particular newspaper did not guard this nest from harm. It saw the egg and probably the chick, but not the fledgeling. A

murderous deed was committed above the public
highway, but whether in the open day or under
cover of darkness I have no means of knowing.
The frisky red squirrel was doubtless the culprit.
The other nest was in a maple sapling, within a
few yards of the little rustic summer-house already
referred to.   The first attempt of the season, I
suspect, had failed in a more secluded place under
the hill; so the pair had come up nearer the house
for protection.   The male sang in the trees near by
for several days before I chanced to see the nest.
The very morning, I think, it was finished, I saw a
red squirrel exploring a tree but a few yards away;
he probably knew what the singing meant as well
as I did.   I did not see the inside of the nest, for
it was almost instantly deserted, the female having
probably laid a single egg, which the squirrel had
devoured.

If I were a bird, in building my nest I should
follow the example of the bobolink, placing it in
the midst of a broad meadow, where there was no
spear of grass, or flower, or growth unlike another
to mark its site.   I judge that the bobolink escapes
the dangers to which I have adverted as few or no
other birds do.   Unless the mowers come along at
an earlier date than she has anticipated, that is,
before July 1st, or a skunk goes nosing through
the grass, which is unusual, she is as safe as bird
well can be in the great open of nature.   She
selects the most monotonous and uniform place she
can find amid the daisies or the timothy and clover,

particular meadow-lily, I walked straight to the
spot, bent down, and gazed long and intently into
the grass.   Finally my eye separated the nest and
its young from its surroundings.   My foot had
barely missed them in my search, but by how much
they had escaped my eye I could not tell.   Probably not by distance at all, but simply by unrecogni-
tion.   They were virtually invisible.   The dark
gray and yellowish brown dry grass and stubble of
the meadow-bottom were exactly copied in the color
of the half-fledged young.   More than that, they
hugged the nest so closely and formed such a compact mass, that though there were five of them,
they preserved the unit of expression, — no single
head or form was defined; they were one, and that
one was without shape or color, and not separable,
except by closest scrutiny, from the one of the
meadow-bottom.   That nest prospered, as bobolinks'
nests doubtless generally do; for, notwithstanding
the enormous slaughter of the birds during their
fall migrations by Southern sportsmen, the bobolink appears to hold its own, and its music does not
diminish in our Northern meadows.

Birds with whom the struggle for life is the
sharpest seem to be more prolific than those whose
nest and young are exposed to fewer dangers.   The
robin, the sparrow, the pewee, etc., will rear, or
make the attempt to rear, two and sometimes three
broods in a season; but the bobolink, the oriole,
the kingbird, the goldfinch, the cedar-bird, the
birds of prey, and the woodpeckers, that build in

safe retreats in the trunks of trees, have usually but
a single brood. If the bobolink reared two broods,
our meadows would swarm with them.

I noted three nests of the cedar-bird in August
in a single orchard, all productive, but each with
one or more unfruitful eggs in it. The cedar-bird
is the most silent of our birds, having but a single
fine note, so far as I have observed, but its manners
are very expressive at times. No bird known to
me is capable of expressing so much silent alarm
while on the nest as this bird. As you ascend the
tree and draw near it, it depresses its plumage and
crest, stretches up its neck, and becomes the very
picture of fear. Other birds, under like circumstances, hardly change their expression at all till
they launch into the air, when by their voice they
express anger rather than alarm.

I have referred to the red squirrel as a destroyer
of the eggs and young of birds. I think the mischief it does in this respect can hardly be overesti-
mated. Nearly all birds look upon it as their
enemy, and attack and annoy it when it appears
near their breeding haunts. Thus, I have seen the
pewee, the cuckoo, the robin, and the wood thrush
pursuing it with angry voice and gestures. A
friend of mine saw a pair of robins attack one in the
top of a tall tree so vigorously that they caused it
to lose its hold, when it fell to the ground, and
was so stunned by the blow as to allow him to pick
it up. If you wish the birds to breed and thrive
in your orchard and groves, kill every red squirrel

that infests the place; kill every weasel also. The
weasel is a subtle and arch enemy of the birds. It
climbs trees and explores them with great ease and
nimbleness. I have seen it do so on several occasions. One day my attention was arrested by the
angry notes of a pair of brown thrashers that were
flitting from bush to bush along an old stone row
in a remote field. Presently I saw what it was
that excited them, — three large red weasels, or
ermines, coming along the stone wall, and leisurely
and half playfully exploring every tree that stood
near it. They had probably robbed the thrashers.
They would go up the trees with great ease, and
glide serpent-like out upon the main branches.
When they descended the tree they were unable to
come straight down, like a squirrel, but went around
it spirally. How boldly they thrust their heads
out of the wall, and eyed me and sniffed me as I
drew near, — their round, thin ears, their prominent, glistening, bead-like eyes, and the curving,
snake-like motions of the head and neck being very
noticeable. They looked like blood-suckers and
egg-suckers. They suggested something extremely
remorseless and cruel. One could understand the
alarm of the rats when they discover one of these
fearless, subtle, and circumventing creatures thread-
ing their holes. To flee must be like trying to
escape death itself. I was one day standing in the
woods upon a flat stone, in what at certain seasons
was the bed of a stream, when one of these weasels

the last degree.   The foot sped through it without
hindrance.   I fancied the grouse and quails quietly
sitting down in the open places, and letting it drift
over them.   With head under wing, and wing
snugly folded, they would be softly and tenderly
buried in a few moments.   The mice and the squirrels were in their dens, but I fancied the fox asleep
upon some rock or log, and allowing the flakes to
cover him.   The hare in her form, too, was being
warmly sepulchred with the rest.   I thought of the
young cattle and the sheep huddled together on the
lee side of a haystack in some remote field, all enveloped in mantles of white.

> " I thought me on the ourie cattle,
>   Or silly sheep, wha bide this brattle
>   O' wintry war,
>   Or thro' the drift, deep-lairing sprattle,
>   Beneath a scaur.
>
> " Ilk happing bird, wee helpless thing,
>   That in the merry months o' spring
>   Delighted me to hear thee sing,
>   What comes o' thee ?
>   Where wilt thou cow'r thy chittering wing,
>   And close thy ee ? "

As I passed the creek, I noticed the white woolly
masses that filled the water.   It was as if somebody
upstream had been washing his sheep and the water
had carried away all the wool, and I thought of the
Psalmist's phrase, "He giveth snow like wool."
On the river a heavy fall of snow simulates a thin
layer of cotton batting.   The tide drifts it along,
and, where it meets with an obstruction alongshore,
it folds up and becomes wrinkled or convoluted like

a fabric, or like cotton sheeting. Attempt to row
a boat through it, and it seems indeed like cotton
or wool, every fibre of which resists your progress.

As the sun went down and darkness fell, the
storm impulse reached its full. It became a wild
conflagration of wind and snow; the world was
wrapt in frost flame; it enveloped one, and penetrated his lungs and caught away his breath like a
blast from a burning city. How it whipped around
and under every cover and searched out every crack
and crevice, sifting under the shingles in the attic,
darting its white tongue under the kitchen door,
puffing its breath down the chimney, roaring through
the woods, stalking like a sheeted ghost across the
hills, bending in white and ever-changing forms
above the fences, sweeping across the plains, whirl-
ing in eddies behind the buildings, or leaping spite-
fully up their walls, — in short, taking the world
entirely to itself, and giving a loose rein to its
desire.

But in the morning, behold! the world was not
consumed; it was not the besom of destruction,
after all, but the gentle hand of mercy. How
deeply and warmly and spotlessly Earth's nakedness
is clothed! — the "wool" of the Psalmist nearly
two feet deep. And as far as warmth and protection are concerned, there is a good deal of the
virtue of wool in such a snow-fall. How it protects the grass, the plants, the roots of the trees,
and the worms, insects, and smaller animals in the
ground! It is a veritable fleece, beneath which the

shivering earth ("the frozen hills ached with pain,"
says one of our young poets) is restored to warmth.
When the temperature of the air is at zero, the
thermometer, placed at the surface of the ground
beneath a foot and a half of snow, would probably
indicate but a few degrees below freezing; the snow
is rendered such a perfect non-conductor of heat
mainly by reason of the quantity of air that is
caught and retained between the crystals.   Then
how, like a fleece of wool, it rounds and fills out
the landscape, and makes the leanest and most
angular field look smooth!

The day dawned, and continued as innocent and
fair as the day which had preceded, — two mountain-
peaks of sky and sun, with their valley of cloud
and snow between.   Walk to the nearest spring
run on such a morning, and you can see the Colo-
rado valley and the great cañons of the West in
miniature, carved in alabaster.   In the midst of
the plain of snow lie these chasms; the vertical
walls, the bold headlands, the turrets and spires
and obelisks, the rounded and towering capes, the
carved and buttressed precipices, the branch valleys
and cañons, and the winding and tortuous course
of the main channel are all here, — all that the
Yosemite or Yellowstone have to show, except the
terraces and the cascades.   Sometimes my cañon
is bridged, and one's fancy runs nimbly across a
vast arch of Parian marble, and that makes up for
the falls and the terraces.   Where the ground is
marshy, I come upon a pretty and vivid illustration

gry, for rats and squirrels and mice and birds are
everywhere.   They probably do not fall a prey to
any other animal, and very rarely to man.   But
the circumstances or agencies that check the increase
of any species of animal or bird are, as Darwin
says, very obscure and but little known.

V

A SNOW-STORM

THAT is a striking line with which Emerson opens his beautiful poem of the Snow-Storm: —

> " Announced by all the trumpets of the sky,
> Arrives the snow, and, driving o'er the fields,
> Seems nowhere to alight."

One seems to see the clouds puffing their cheeks as they sound the charge of their white legions. But the line is more accurately descriptive of a rainstorm, as, in both summer and winter, rain is usually preceded by wind. Homer, describing a snow-storm in his time, says: —

> " The winds are lulled."

The preparations of a snow-storm are, as a rule, gentle and quiet; a marked hush pervades both the earth and the sky. The movements of the celestial forces are muffled, as if the snow already paved the way of their coming. There is no uproar, no clashing of arms, no blowing of wind trumpets. These soft, feathery, exquisite crystals are formed as if in the silence and privacy of the inner cloud-chambers. Rude winds would break the spell and mar the process. The clouds are smoother, and slower in their movements, with less definite outlines than

VI

A TASTE OF MAINE BIRCH

THE traveler and camper-out in Maine, unless he penetrates its more northern portions, has less reason to remember it as a pine-tree State than a birch-tree State. The white-pine forests have melted away like snow in the spring and gone downstream, leaving only patches here and there in the more remote and inaccessible parts. The portion of the State I saw — the valley of the Kennebec and the woods about Moxie Lake — had been shorn of its pine timber more than forty years before, and is now covered with a thick growth of spruce and cedar and various deciduous trees. But the birch abounds. Indeed, when the pine goes out the birch comes in; the race of men succeeds the race of giants. This tree has great stay-at-home virtues. Let the sombre, aspiring, mysterious pine go; the birch has humble, every-day uses. In Maine, the paper or canoe birch is turned to more account than any other tree. I read in Gibbon that the natives of ancient Assyria used to celebrate in verse or prose the three hundred and sixty uses to which the various parts and products of the palm-tree were applied. The Maine birch is turned to so many accounts that it may well be called the palm of this region. Uncle Nathan, our guide, said it was made especially for the camper-out; yes, and for the woodman and frontiersman generally. It is a magazine, a furnishing store set up in the wilderness, whose goods are free to every comer. The whole equipment of the camp lies folded in it, and comes forth at the beck of the woodman's axe: tent, water-proof roof, boat, camp utensils, buckets, cups, plates, spoons, napkins, table-cloths, paper for letters or your journal, torches, candles, kindling-wood, and fuel. The canoe birch yields you its vestments with the utmost liberality. Ask for its coat, and it gives you its waistcoat also. Its bark seems wrapped about it layer upon layer, and comes off with great ease. We saw many rude structures and cabins shingled and sided with it, and haystacks capped with it. Near a maple-sugar camp there was a large pile of birch-bark sap-buckets, — each bucket made of a piece of bark about a yard square, folded up as the tinman folds up a sheet of tin to make a square vessel, the corners bent around against the sides and held by a wooden pin. When, one day, we were overtaken by a shower in traveling through the woods, our guide quickly stripped large sheets of the bark from a near tree, and we had each a perfect umbrella as by magic. When the rain was over, and we moved on, I wrapped mine about me like a large leather apron, and it shielded my clothes from the wet bushes. When we came to a spring, Uncle Nathan

would have a birch-bark cup ready before any of us
could get a tin one out of his knapsack, and I think
water never tasted so sweet as from one of these
bark cups. It is exactly the thing. It just fits
the mouth, and it seems to give new virtues to the
water. It makes me thirsty now when I think of
it. In our camp at Moxie, we made a large birch-
bark box to keep the butter in; and the butter in
this box, covered with some leafy boughs, I think
improved in flavor day by day. Maine butter needs
something to mollify and sweeten it a little, and I
think birch bark will do it. In camp Uncle Nathan
often drank his tea and coffee from a bark cup; the
china closet in the birch-tree was always handy,
and our vulgar tinware was generally a good deal
mixed, and the kitchen maid not at all particular
about dish-washing. We all tried the oatmeal with
the maple syrup in one of these dishes, and the
stewed mountain cranberries, using a birch-bark
spoon, and never found service better. Uncle Nathan declared he could boil potatoes in a bark kettle, and I did not doubt him. Instead of sending
our soiled napkins and table-spreads to the wash,
we rolled them up into candles and torches, and
drew daily upon our stores in the forest for new
ones.

But the great triumph of the birch is, of course,
the bark canoe. When Uncle Nathan took us out
under his little woodshed, and showed us, or rather
modestly permitted us to see, his nearly finished
canoe, it was like a first glimpse of some new and

unknown genius of the woods or streams. It sat
there on the chips and shavings and fragments of
bark like some shy, delicate creature just emerged
from its hiding-place, or like some wild flower just
opened. It was the first boat of the kind I had
ever seen, and it filled my eye completely. What
woodcraft it indicated, and what a wild, free life,
sylvan life, it promised! It had such a fresh,
aboriginal look as I had never before seen in any
kind of handiwork. Its clear, yellow-red color
would have become the cheek of an Indian maiden.
Then its supple curves and swells, its sinewy stays
and thwarts, its bow-like contour, its tomahawk
stem and stern rising quickly and sharply from its
frame, were all vividly suggestive of the race from
which it came. An old Indian had taught Uncle
Nathan the art, and the soul of the ideal red man
looked out of the boat before us. Uncle Nathan
had spent two days ranging the mountains looking
for a suitable tree, and had worked nearly a week
on the craft. It was twelve feet long, and would
seat and carry five men nicely. Three trees con-
tribute to the making of a canoe beside the birch,
namely, the white cedar for ribs and lining, the
spruce for roots and fibres to sew its joints and bind
its frame, and the pine for pitch or rosin to stop
its seams and cracks. It is hand-made and home-
made, or rather wood-made, in a sense that no
other craft is, except a dugout, and it suggests a
taste and a refinement that few products of civilization realize. The design of a savage, it yet looks

like the thought of a poet, and its grace and fitness
haunt the imagination.   I suppose its production
was the inevitable result of the Indian's wants and
surroundings, but that does not detract from its
beauty.   It is, indeed, one of the fairest flowers
the thorny plant of necessity ever bore.   Our
canoe, as I have intimated, was not yet finished
when we first saw it, nor yet when we took it up,
with its architect, upon our metaphorical backs and
bore it to the woods.   It lacked part of its cedar
lining and the rosin upon its joints, and these were
added after we reached our destination.

Though we were not indebted to the birch-tree
for our guide, Uncle Nathan, as he was known in
all that country, yet he matched well these woodsy
products and conveniences.   The birch-tree had
given him a large part of his tuition, and, kneeling
in his canoe and making it shoot noiselessly over
the water with that subtle yet indescribably expressive and athletic play of the muscles of the back
and shoulders, the boat and the man seemed born
of the same spirit.   He had been a hunter and
trapper for over forty years; he had grown gray in
the woods, had ripened and matured there, and
everything about him was as if the spirit of the
woods had had the ordering of it; his whole make-
up was in a minor and subdued key, like the moss
and the lichens, or like the protective coloring of
the game, — everything but his quick sense and
penetrative glance.   He was as gentle and modest
as a girl; his sensibilities were like plants that grow

in the shade. The woods and the solitudes had
touched him with their own softening and refining
influence; had, indeed, shed upon his soil of life a
rich, deep leaf mould that was delightful, and that
nursed, half concealed, the tenderest and wildest
growths. There was grit enough back of and beneath it all, but he presented none of the rough and
repelling traits of character of the conventional
backwoodsman. In the spring he was a driver of
logs on the Kennebec, usually having charge of a
large gang of men; in the winter he was a solitary
trapper and hunter in the forests.

Our first glimpse of Maine waters was Pleasant
Pond, which we found by following a white, rapid,
musical stream from the Kennebec three miles back
into the mountains. Maine waters are for the most
part dark-complexioned, Indian-colored streams, but
Pleasant Pond is a pale-face among them both in
name and nature. It is the only strictly silver
lake I ever saw. Its waters seem almost artificially
white and brilliant, though of remarkable transparency. I think I detected minute shining motes
held in suspension in it. As for the trout, they are
veritable bars of silver until you have cut their
flesh, when they are the reddest of gold. They
have no crimson or other spots, and the straight
lateral line is but a faint pencil-mark. They appeared to be a species of lake trout peculiar to these
waters, uniformly from ten to twelve inches in
length. And these beautiful fish, at the time of
our visit (last of August) at least, were to be taken

only in deep water upon a hook baited with salt pork. And then you needed a letter of introduction to them. They were not to be tempted or cajoled by strangers. We did not succeed in raising a fish, although instructed how it was to be done, until one of the natives, a young and obliging farmer living hard by, came and lent his countenance to the enterprise. I sat in one end of the boat and he in the other, my pork was the same as his, and I manœuvred it as directed, and yet those fish knew his hook from mine in sixty feet of water, and preferred it four times in five. Evidently they did not bite because they were hungry, but solely for old acquaintance' sake.

Pleasant Pond is an irregular sheet of water, two miles or more in its greatest diameter, with high rugged mountains rising up from its western shore, and low rolling hills sweeping back from its eastern and northern, covered by a few sterile farms. I was never tired, when the wind was still, of floating along its margin and gazing down into its marvelously translucent depths. The bowlders and fragments of rocks were seen, at a depth of twenty-five or thirty feet, strewing its floor, and apparently as free from any covering of sediment as when they were dropped there by the old glaciers æons ago. Our camp was amid a dense grove of second growth of white pine on the eastern shore, where, for one, I found a most admirable cradle in a little depression outside of the tent, carpeted with pine needles, in which to pass the night. The camper-

out is always in luck if he can find, sheltered by
the trees, a soft hole in the ground, even if he has
a stone for a pillow. The earth must open its
arms a little for us even in life, if we are to sleep
well upon its bosom. I have often heard my grandfather, who was a soldier of the Revolution, tell
with great gusto how he once bivouacked in a little
hollow made by the overturning of a tree, and slept
so soundly that he did not wake up till his cradle
was half full of water from a passing shower.

What bird or other creature might represent the
divinity of Pleasant Pond I do not know, but its
demon, as of most northern inland waters, is the
loon; and a very good demon he is, too, suggesting
something not so much malevolent as arch, sar-
donic, ubiquitous, circumventing, with just a tinge
of something inhuman and uncanny. His fiery-red
eyes gleaming forth from that jet-black head are full
of meaning. Then his strange horse-laughter by
day, and his weird, doleful cry at night, like that
of a lost and wandering spirit, recall no other bird
or beast. He suggests something almost supernatu-
ral in his alertness and amazing quickness, cheating
the shot and the bullet of the sportsman out of
their aim. I know of but one other bird so quick,
and that is the hummingbird, which I never have
been able to kill with a gun. The loon laughs the
shotgun to scorn, and the obliging young farmer
above referred to told me he had shot at them
hundreds of times with his rifle, without effect, —
they always dodged his bullet. We had in our

party a breech-loading rifle, which weapon is perhaps an appreciable moment of time quicker than the ordinary muzzle-loader, and this the poor loon could not or did not dodge. He had not timed himself to that species of firearms, and when, with his fellow, he swam about within rifle range of our camp, letting off volleys of his wild, ironical *ha-ha*, he little suspected the dangerous gun that was matched against him. As the rifle cracked, both loons made the gesture of diving, but only one of them disappeared beneath the water; and when he came to the surface in a few moments, a hundred or more yards away, and saw his companion did not follow, but was floating on the water where he had last seen him, he took the alarm and sped away in the distance. The bird I had killed was a magnificent specimen, and I looked him over with great interest. His glossy checkered coat, his banded neck, his snow-white breast, his powerful lance-shaped beak, his red eyes, his black, thin, slender, marvelously delicate feet and legs, issuing from his muscular thighs, and looking as if they had never touched the ground, his strong wings well forward, while his legs were quite at the apex, and the neat, elegant model of the entire bird, speed and quickness and strength stamped upon every feature, — all delighted and lingered in the eye. The loon appears like anything but a silly bird, unless you see him in some collection, or in the shop of the taxidermist, where he usually looks very tame and goose-like. Nature never meant the loon to stand up, or to use his feet and legs for other purposes than swimming. Indeed, he cannot stand except upon his tail in a perpendicular attitude; but in the collections he is poised upon his feet like a barn-yard fowl, all the wildness and grace and alertness gone out of him. My specimen sits upon a table as upon the surface of the water, his feet trailing behind him, his body low and trim, his head elevated and slightly turned as if in the act of bringing that fiery eye to bear upon you, and vigilance and power stamped upon every lineament.

The loon is to the fishes what the hawk is to the birds; he swoops down to unknown depths upon them, and not even the wary trout can elude him. Uncle Nathan said he had seen the loon disappear, and in a moment come up with a large trout, which he would cut in two with his strong beak and swallow piecemeal. Neither the loon nor the otter can bolt a fish under the water; he must come to the surface to dispose of it. (I once saw a man eat a cake under water in London.) Our guide told me he had seen the parent loon swimming with a single young one upon its back. When closely pressed, it dived, or "div," as he would have it, and left the young bird sitting upon the water. Then it too disappeared, and when the old one returned and called it came out from the shore. On the wing overhead the loon looks not unlike a very large duck, but when it alights it plows into the water like a bombshell. It probably cannot take flight from the land, as the one Gilbert

White saw and describes in his letters was picked up in a field, unable to launch itself into the air.

From Pleasant Pond we went seven miles through the woods to Moxie Lake, following an overgrown lumberman's "tote" road, our canoe and supplies, etc., hauled on a sled by the young farmer with his three-year-old steers. I doubt if birch-bark ever made a rougher voyage than that. As I watched it above the bushes, the sled and the luggage being hidden, it appeared as if tossed in the wildest and most tempestuous sea. When the bushes closed above it, I felt as if it had gone down, or been broken into a hundred pieces. Billows of rocks and logs, and chasms of creeks and spring runs, kept it rearing and pitching in the most frightful manner. The steers went at a spanking pace; indeed, it was a regular bovine gale; but their driver clung to their side amid the brush and bowlders with desperate tenacity, and seemed to manage them by signs and nudges, for he hardly uttered his orders aloud. But we got through without any serious mishap, passing Mosquito Creek and Mosquito Pond, and flanking Mosquito Mountain, but seeing no mosquitoes, and brought up at dusk at a lumberman's old hay-barn, standing in the midst of a lonely clearing on the shores of Moxie Lake.

Here we passed the night, and were lucky in having a good roof over our heads, for it rained heavily. After we were rolled in our blankets and variously disposed upon the haymow, Uncle Nathan lulled us to sleep by a long and characteristic yarn.

I had asked him, half jocosely, if he believed in "spooks;" but he took my question seriously, and without answering it directly, proceeded to tell us what he himself had known and witnessed. It was, by the way, extremely difficult either to surprise or to steal upon any of Uncle Nathan's private opinions and beliefs about matters and things. He was as shy of all debatable subjects as a fox is of a trap. He usually talked in a circle, just as he hunted moose and caribou, so as not to approach his point too rudely and suddenly. He would keep on the lee side of his interlocutor in spite of all one could do. He was thoroughly good and reliable, but the wild creatures of the woods, in pursuit of which he had spent so much of his life, had taught him a curious gentleness and indirection, and to keep himself in the background; he was careful that you should not scent his opinions upon any subject at all polemic, but he would tell you what he had seen and known. What he had seen and known about spooks was briefly this: In company with a neighbor he was passing the night with an old recluse who lived somewhere in these woods. Their host was an Englishman, who had the reputation of having murdered his wife some years before in another part of the country, and, deserted by his grown-up children, was eking out his days in poverty amid these solitudes. The three men were sleeping upon the floor, with Uncle Nathan

next to a rude partition that divided the cabin into
two rooms. At his head there was a door that
opened into this other apartment. Late at night,
Uncle Nathan said, he awoke and turned over,
and his mind was occupied with various things,
when he heard somebody behind the partition. He
reached over and felt that both of his companions
were in their places beside him, and he was somewhat surprised. The person, or whatever it was,
in the other room moved about heavily, and pulled
the table from its place beside the wall to the middle of the floor. "I was not dreaming," said Uncle
Nathan; "I felt of my eyes twice to make sure,
and they were wide open." Presently the door
opened; he was sensible of the draught upon his
head, and a woman's form stepped heavily past
him; he felt the "swirl" of her skirts as she went
by. Then there was a loud noise in the room, as
if some one had fallen his whole length upon the
floor. "It jarred the house," said he, "and woke
everybody up. I asked old Mr. ―― if he heard
that noise. 'Yes,' said he, 'it was thunder.'
But it was not thunder, I know that;" and then
added, "I was no more afraid than I am this
minute. I never was the least mite afraid in my
life. And my eyes were wide open," he repeated;
"I felt of them twice; but whether that was the
speret of that man's murdered wife or not, I cannot tell. They said she was an uncommon heavy
woman." Uncle Nathan was a man of unusually
quick and acute senses, and he did not doubt their

evidence on this occasion any more than he did
when they prompted him to level his rifle at a bear
or a moose.

Moxie Lake lies much lower than Pleasant Pond,
and its waters compared with those of the latter are
as copper compared with silver. It is very irregular in shape; now narrowing to the dimensions of
a slow-moving grassy creek, then expanding into
a broad deep basin with rocky shores, and command-
ing the noblest mountain scenery. It is rarely that
the pond-lily and the speckled trout are found
together, — the fish the soul of the purest spring
water, the flower the transfigured spirit of the dark
mud and slime of sluggish summer streams and
ponds; yet in Moxie they were both found in perfection. Our camp was amid the birches, poplars,
and white cedars near the head of the lake, where
the best fishing at this season was to be had.
Moxie has a small oval head, rather shallow, but
lumpy with rocks; a long, deep neck, full of
springs, where the trout lie; and a very broad
chest, with two islands tufted with pine-trees for
breasts. We swam in the head, we fished in the
neck, or in a small section of it, a space about the
size of the Adam's apple, and we paddled across
and around the broad expanse below. Our birch-
bark was not finished and christened till we reached
Moxie. The cedar lining was completed at Pleasant Pond, where we had the use of a *bateau*, but
the rosin was not applied to the seams till we
reached this lake. When I knelt down in it for

the first time, and put its slender maple paddle into the water, it sprang away with such quickness and speed that it disturbed me in my seat. I had spurred a more restive and spirited steed than I was used to. In fact, I had never been in a craft that sustained so close a relation to my will, and was so responsive to my slightest wish. When I caught my first large trout from it, it sympathized a little too closely, and my enthusiasm started a leak, which, however, with a live coal and a piece of rosin, was quickly mended. You cannot perform much of a war-dance in a birch-bark canoe; better wait till you get on dry land. Yet as a boat it is not so shy and "ticklish" as I had imagined. One needs to be on the alert, as becomes a sportsman and an angler, and in his dealings with it must charge himself with three things, — precision, moderation, and circumspection.

Trout weighing four and five pounds have been taken at Moxie, but none of that size came to our hand. I realized the fondest hopes I had dared to indulge in when I hooked the first two-pounder of my life, and my extreme solicitude lest he get away I trust was pardonable. My friend, in relating the episode in camp, said I had implored him to row me down in the middle of the lake that I might have room to manœuvre my fish. But the slander has barely a grain of truth in it. The water near us showed several old stakes broken off just below the surface, and my fish was determined to wrap my leader about one of these stakes; it was only

for the clear space a few yards farther out that I
prayed. It was not long after that my friend found
himself in an anxious frame of mind. He hooked
a large trout, which came home on him so suddenly
that he had not time to reel up his line, and in his
extremity he stretched his tall form into the air and
lifted up his pole to an incredible height. He
checked the trout before it got under the boat, but
dared not come down an inch, and then began his
amusing further elongation in reaching for his reel
with one hand, while he carried it ten feet into the
air with the other. A step-ladder would perhaps
have been more welcome to him just then than at
any other moment during his life. But the trout was
saved, though my friend's buttons and suspenders
suffered.

We learned a new trick in fly-fishing here, worth
disclosing. It was not one day in four that the
trout would take the fly on the surface. When
the south wind was blowing and the clouds threat-
ened rain, they would at times, notably about three
o'clock, rise handsomely. But on all other occasions it was rarely that we could entice them up
through the twelve or fifteen feet of water. Earlier
in the season they are not so lazy and indifferent,
but the August languor and drowsiness were now
upon them. So we learned by a lucky accident to
fish deep for them, even weighting our leaders with
a shot, and allowing the flies to sink nearly to the
bottom. After a moment's pause we would draw
them slowly up, and when half or two thirds of

the way to the top the trout would strike, when
the sport became lively enough. Most of our fish
were taken in this way. There is nothing like the
flash and the strike at the surface, and perhaps
only the need of food will ever tempt the genuine
angler into any more prosaic style of fishing; but
if you must go below the surface, a shotted leader
is the best thing to use.

Our camp-fire at night served more purposes than
one; from its embers and flickering shadows, Uncle
Nathan read us many a tale of his life in the woods.
They were the same old hunter's stories, except
that they evidently had the merit of being strictly
true, and hence were not very thrilling or marvel-
ous. Uncle Nathan's tendency was rather to tone
down and belittle his experiences than to exagger-
ate them. If he ever bragged at all (and I suspect
he did just a little, when telling us how he outshot
one of the famous riflemen of the American team,
whom he was guiding through these woods), he did
it in such a sly, roundabout way that it was hard
to catch him at it. His passage with the rifleman
referred to shows the difference between the practi-
cal offhand skill of the hunter in the woods and
the science of the long-range target-hitter. Mr.
Bull's Eye had heard that his guide was a capital
shot, and had seen some proof of it, and hence
could not rest till he had had a trial of skill with
him. Uncle Nathan, being the challenged party,
had the right to name the distance and the conditions. A piece of white paper the size of a silver

dollar was put upon a tree twelve rods off, the con-
testants to fire three shots each offhand. Uncle
Nathan's first bullet barely missed the mark, but
the other two were planted well into it.   Then the
great rifleman took his turn, and missed every time.

"By hemp!" said Uncle Nathan, "I was sorry
I shot so well, Mr. —— took it so to heart; and
I had used his own rifle, too.   He did not get over
it for a week."

But far more ignominious was the failure of Mr.
Bull's Eye when he saw his first bear. . They were
paddling slowly and silently down Dead River,
when the guide heard a slight noise in the bushes
just behind a little bend.   He whispered to the
rifleman, who sat kneeling in the bow of the boat,
to take his rifle.   But instead of doing so, he picked
up his two-barreled shotgun.   As they turned the
point, there stood a bear not twenty yards away,
drinking from the stream.   Uncle Nathan held the
canoe, while the man who had come so far in quest
of this very game was trying to lay down his shotgun and pick up his rifle.   "His hand moved like
the hand of a clock," said Uncle Nathan, "and I
could hardly keep my seat.   I knew the bear would
see us in a moment more and run."   Instead of
laying his gun by his side, where it belonged, he
reached it across in front of him, and laid it upon
his rifle, and in trying to get the latter from under
it a noise was made; the bear heard it and raised
his head.   Still there was time, for as the bear
sprang into the woods he stopped and looked back,

— "as I knew he would," said the guide; yet the marksman was not ready. "By hemp! I could have shot three bears," exclaimed Uncle Nathan, "while he was getting that rifle to his face!"

Poor Mr. Bull's Eye was deeply humiliated. "Just the chance I had been looking for," he said, "and my wits suddenly left me."

As a hunter, Uncle Nathan always took the game on its own terms, that of still-hunting. He even shot foxes in this way, going into the fields in the fall just at break of day, and watching for them about their mousing haunts. One morning, by these tactics, he shot a black fox; a fine specimen, he said, and a wild one, for he stopped and looked and listened every few yards.

He had killed over two hundred moose, a large number of them at night on the lakes. His method was to go out in his canoe and conceal himself by some point or island, and wait till he heard the game. In the fall the moose comes into the water to eat the large fibrous roots of the pond-lilies. He splashes along till he finds a suitable spot, when he begins feeding, sometimes thrusting his head and neck several feet under water. The hunter listens, and when the moose lifts his head and the rills of water run from it, and he hears him "swash" the lily roots about to get off the mud, it is his time to start. Silently as a shadow he creeps up on the moose, who, by the way, it seems, never expects the approach of danger from the water side. If the hunter accidentally makes a noise, the moose

looks toward the shore for it. There is always
a slight gleam on the water, Uncle Nathan says,
even in the darkest night, and the dusky form of
the moose can be distinctly seen upon it. When
the hunter sees this darker shadow, he lifts his gun
to the sky and gets the range of its barrels, then
lowers it till it covers the mark, and fires.

The largest moose Uncle Nathan ever killed is
mounted in the State House at Augusta. He shot
him while hunting in winter on snow-shoes. The
moose was reposing upon the ground, with his head
stretched out in front of him, as one may sometimes
see a cow resting. The position was such that only
a quartering shot through the animal's hip could
reach its heart. Studying the problem carefully,
and taking his own time, the hunter fired. The
moose sprang into the air, turned, and came with
tremendous strides straight toward him. "I knew
he had not seen or scented me," said Uncle Nathan, "but, by hemp, I wished myself somewhere
else just then; for I was lying right down in his
path." But the noble animal stopped a few yards
short, and fell dead with a bullet hole through his
heart.

When the moose yard in the winter, that is,
restrict their wanderings to a well-defined section
of the forest or mountain, trampling down the snow
and beating paths in all directions, they browse off
only the most dainty morsels first; when they go
over the ground a second time they crop a little
cleaner; the third time they sort still closer, till

by and by nothing is left. Spruce, hemlock, poplar, the barks of various trees, everything within reach, is cropped close. When the hunter comes upon one of these yards the problem for him to settle is, Where are the moose? for it is absolutely necessary that he keep on the lee side of them. So he considers the lay of the land, the direction of the wind, the time of day, the depth of the snow, examines the spoor, the cropped twigs, and studies every hint and clew like a detective. Uncle Nathan said he could not explain to another how he did it, but he could usually tell in a few minutes in what direction to look for the game. His experience had ripened into a kind of intuition or winged reasoning that was above rules.

He said that most large game, — deer, caribou, moose, bear, — when started by the hunter and not much scared, were sure to stop and look back before disappearing from sight; he usually waited for this last and best chance to fire. He told us of a huge bear he had seen one morning while still-hunting foxes in the fields; the bear saw him, and got into the woods before he could get a good shot. In her course, some distance up the mountain, was a bald, open spot, and he felt sure when she crossed this spot she would pause and look behind her; and sure enough, like Lot's wife, her curiosity got the better of her; she stopped to have a final look, and her travels ended there and then.

Uncle Nathan had trapped and shot a great many bears, and some of his experiences revealed an un-

usual degree of sagacity in this animal. One April,
when the weather began to get warm and thawy,
an old bear left her den in the rocks, and built a
large, warm nest of grass, leaves, and the bark of
the white cedar, under a tall balsam fir that stood
in a low, sunny, open place amid the mountains.
Hither she conducted her two cubs, and the family
began life in what might be called their spring resi-
dence. The tree above them was for shelter, and
for refuge for the cubs in case danger approached,
as it soon did in the form of Uncle Nathan. He
happened that way soon after the bear had moved.
Seeing her track in the snow, he concluded to follow it. When the bear had passed, the snow had
been soft and sposhy, and she had "slumped," he
said, several inches. It was now hard and slippery.
As he neared the tree, the track turned and doubled,
and tacked this way and that, and led through the
worst brush and brambles to be found. This was
a shrewd thought of the old bear; she could thus
hear her enemy coming a long time before he drew
very near. When Uncle Nathan finally reached the
nest, he found it empty, but still warm. Then he
began to circle about and look for the bear's footprints or nailprints upon the frozen snow. Not finding them the first time, he took a larger circle, then
a still larger; finally he made a long détour, and
spent nearly an hour searching for some clew to the
direction the bear had taken, but all to no purpose.
Then he returned to the tree and scrutinized it.
The foliage was very dense, but presently he made

out one of the cubs near the top, standing up amid the branches, and peering down at him. This he killed. Further search only revealed a mass of foliage apparently more dense than usual, but a bullet sent into it was followed by loud whimpering and crying, and the other baby bear came tumbling down. In leaving the place, greatly puzzled as to what had become of the mother bear, Uncle Nathan followed another of her frozen tracks, and after about a quarter of a mile saw beside it, upon the snow, the fresh trail he had been in search of. In making her escape, the bear had stepped exactly in her old tracks that were hard and icy, and had thus left no mark till she took to the snow again.

During his trapping expeditions into the woods in midwinter, I was curious to know how Uncle Nathan passed the nights, as we were twice pinched with the cold at that season in our tent and blankets. It was no trouble to keep warm, he said, in the coldest weather. As night approached, he would select a place for his camp on the side of a hill. With one of his snow-shoes he would shovel out the snow till the ground was reached, carrying the snow out in front, as we scrape the earth out of the side of a hill to level up a place for the house and yard. On this level place, which, however, was made to incline slightly toward the hill, his bed of boughs was made. On the ground he had uncovered he built his fire. His bed was thus on a level with the fire, and the heat could not thaw the snow under him and let him down, or the burn-

ing logs roll upon him. With a steep ascent behind
it, the fire burned better, and the wind was not so
apt to drive the smoke and blaze in upon him.
Then, with the long, curving branches of the spruce
stuck thickly around three sides of the bed, and
curving over and uniting their tops above it, a
shelter was formed that would keep out the cold
and the snow, and that would catch and retain the
warmth of the fire. Rolled in his blanket in such
a nest, Uncle Nathan had passed hundreds of the
most frigid winter nights.

One day we made an excursion of three miles
through the woods to Bald Mountain, following a
dim trail. We saw, as we filed silently along,
plenty of signs of caribou, deer, and bear, but were
not blessed with a sight of either of the animals
themselves. I noticed that Uncle Nathan, in looking through the woods, did not hold his head as
we did, but thrust it slightly forward, and peered
under the branches like a deer, or other wild creature.

The summit of Bald Mountain was the most
impressive mountain-top I had ever seen, mainly,
perhaps, because it was one enormous crown of
nearly naked granite. The rock had that gray,
elemental, eternal look which granite alone has.
One seemed to be face to face with the gods of the
fore-world. Like an atom, like a breath of to-day,
we were suddenly confronted by abysmal geologic
time, — the eternities past and the eternities to
come. The enormous cleavage of the rocks, the

appalling cracks and fissures, the rent bowlders, the
smitten granite floors, gave one a new sense of the
power of heat and frost. In one place we noticed
several deep parallel grooves, made by the old glaciers. In the depressions on the summit there was
a hard, black, peaty-like soil that looked indescribably ancient and unfamiliar. Out of this mould,
which might have come from the moon or the inter-
planetary spaces, were growing mountain cranberries and blueberries or huckleberries. We were
soon so absorbed in gathering the latter that we
were quite oblivious of the grandeurs about us. It
is these blueberries that attract the bears. In eating them, Uncle Nathan said, they take the bushes
in their mouths, and by an upward movement strip
them clean of both leaves and berries. We were
constantly on the lookout for the bears, but failed
to see any. Yet a few days afterward, when two
of our party returned here and encamped upon the
mountain, they saw five during their stay, but failed
to get a good shot. The rifle was in the wrong
place each time. The man with the shotgun saw
an old bear and two cubs lift themselves from behind a rock and twist their noses around for his
scent, and then shrink away. They were too far
off for his buckshot. I must not forget the superb
view that lay before us, a wilderness of woods and
waters stretching away to the horizon on every
hand. Nearly a dozen lakes and ponds could be
seen, and in a clearer atmosphere the foot of Moose-
head Lake would have been visible. The highest

and most striking mountain to be seen was Mount
Bigelow, rising above Dead River, far to the west,
and its two sharp peaks notching the horizon like
enormous saw-teeth. We walked around and viewed
curiously a huge bowlder on the top of the mountain that had been split in two vertically, and one
of the halves moved a few feet out of its bed.   It
looked recent and familiar, but suggested gods instead of men.   The force that moved the rock had
plainly come from the north.   I thought of a similar bowlder I had seen not long before on the highest point of the Shawangunk Mountains, in New
York, one side of which is propped up with a large
stone, as wall-builders prop up a rock to wrap a
chain around it.   The rock seems poised lightly,
and has but a few points of bearing.   In this instance, too, the power had come from the north.

The prettiest botanical specimen my trip yielded
was a little plant that bears the ugly name of
horned bladderwort, and which I found growing in
marshy places along the shores of Moxie Lake.
It has a slender, naked stem nearly a foot high,
crowned by two or more large deep yellow flowers,
— flowers the shape of little bonnets or hoods.
One almost expected to see tiny faces looking out
of them.   This illusion is heightened by the horn
or spur of the flower, which projects from the hood
like a long tapering chin, — some masker's device.
Then the cape behind, — what a smart upward
curve it has, as if spurned by the fairy shoulders
it was meant to cover!   But perhaps the most

notable thing about the flower was its fragrance, —
the richest and strongest perfume I have ever found
in a wild flower. This our botanist, Gray, does
not mention, as if one should describe the lark and
forget its song. The fragrance suggested that of
white clover, but was more rank and spicy.

The woods about Moxie Lake were literally carpeted with linnæa. I had never seen it in such
profusion. In early summer, the period of its
bloom, what a charming spectacle the mossy floors
of these remote woods must present! The flowers
are purple rose-color, nodding and fragrant. Another very abundant plant in these woods was the
Clintonia borealis. Uncle Nathan said it was
called "bear's corn," though he did not know why.
The only noticeable flower by the Maine roadsides
at this season that is not common in other parts of
the country is the harebell. Its bright blue, bell-
shaped corolla shone out from amid the dry grass
and weeds all along the route. It was one of the
most delicate roadside flowers I had ever seen.

The only new bird I saw in Maine was the
pileated woodpecker, or black "log-cock," called by
Uncle Nathan "woodcock." I had never before
seen or heard this bird, and its loud cackle in the
woods about Moxie was a new sound to me. It is
the wildest and largest of our northern woodpeckers,
and the rarest. Its voice and the sound of its
hammer are heard only in the depths of the northern woods. It is about as large as a crow, and
nearly as black.

We stayed a week at Moxie, or until we became surfeited with its trout, and had killed the last merganser duck that lingered about our end of the lake. The trout that had accumulated on our hands we had kept alive in a large champagne basket submerged in the lake, and the morning we broke camp the basket was towed to the shore and opened ; and after we had feasted our eyes upon the superb spectacle, every trout — there were twelve or fifteen, some of them two-pounders — was allowed to swim back into the lake. They went leisurely, in couples and in trios, and were soon kicking up their heels in their old haunts. I expect that the divinity who presides over Moxie will see to it that every one of those trout, doubled in weight, comes to our basket in the future.

VII

THE country is more of a wilderness, more of a
wild solitude, in the winter than in the summer. The wild comes out. The urban, the cultivated, is hidden or negatived. You shall hardly
know a good field from a poor, a meadow from a
pasture, a park from a forest. Lines and boundaries are disregarded; gates and bar-ways are
unclosed; man lets go his hold upon the earth;
title-deeds are deep buried beneath the snow; the
best-kept grounds relapse to a state of nature;
under the pressure of the cold, all the wild creatures
become outlaws, and roam abroad beyond their usual
haunts. The partridge comes to the orchard for
buds; the rabbit comes to the garden and lawn;
the crows and jays come to the ash-heap and corn-
crib, the snow buntings to the stack and to the barn-
yard; the sparrows pilfer from the domestic fowls;
the pine grosbeak comes down from the north and
shears your maples of their buds; the fox prowls
about your premises at night; and the red squirrels
find your grain in the barn or steal the butternuts
from your attic. In fact, winter, like some great
calamity, changes the status of most creatures and

sets them adrift. Winter, like poverty, makes us acquainted with strange bedfellows.

For my part, my nearest approach to a strange bedfellow is the little gray rabbit that has taken up her abode under my study floor. As she spends the day here and is out larking at night, she is not much of a bedfellow, after all. It is probable that I disturb her slumbers more than she does mine. I think she is some support to me under there, — a silent, wide-eyed witness and backer; a type of the gentle and harmless in savage nature. She has no sagacity to give me or lend me, but that soft, nimble foot of hers, and that touch as of cotton wherever she goes, are worthy of emulation. I think I can feel her good-will through the floor, and I hope she can mine. When I have a happy thought, I imagine her ears twitch, especially when I think of the sweet apple I will place by her doorway at night. I wonder if that fox chanced to catch a glimpse of her the other night when he stealthily leaped over the fence near by and walked along between the study and the house? How clearly one could read that it was not a little dog that had passed there! There was something furtive in the track; it shied off away from the house and around it, as if eying it suspiciously; and then it had the caution and deliberation of the fox, — bold, bold, but not too bold; wariness was in every footprint. If it had been a little dog that had chanced to wander that way, when he crossed my path he would have followed it up to the barn and have gone smelling around for a bone; but this sharp, cautious track held straight across all others, keeping five or six rods from the house, up the hill, across the highway toward a neighboring farm-stead, with its nose in the air, and its eye and ear alert, so to speak.

A winter neighbor of mine, in whom I am interested, and who perhaps lends me his support after his kind, is a little red owl, whose retreat is in the heart of an old apple-tree just over the fence. Where he keeps himself in spring and summer, I do not know, but late every fall, and at intervals all winter, his hiding-place is discovered by the jays and nuthatches, and proclaimed from the tree-tops for the space of half an hour or so, with all the powers of voice they can command. Four times during one winter they called me out to behold this little ogre feigning sleep in his den, sometimes in one apple-tree, sometimes in another. Whenever I heard their cries, I knew my neighbor was being berated. The birds would take turns at looking in upon him, and uttering their alarm-notes. Every jay within hearing would come to the spot, and at once approach the hole in the trunk or limb, and with a kind of breathless eagerness and excitement take a peep at the owl, and then join the outcry. When I approached they would hastily take a final look, and then withdraw and regard my movements intently. After accustoming my eye to the faint light of the cavity for a few moments, I could usually make out the owl at the bottom feigning sleep. Feigning, I say, because this is what he really did, as I first discovered one day when I cut into his retreat with the axe. The loud blows and the falling chips did not disturb him at all. When I reached in a stick and pulled him over on his side, leaving one of his wings spread out, he made no attempt to recover himself, but lay among the chips and fragments of decayed wood, like a part of themselves. Indeed, it took a sharp eye to distinguish him. Not till I had pulled him forth by one wing, rather rudely, did he abandon his trick of simulated sleep or death. Then, like a detected pickpocket, he was suddenly transformed into another creature. His eyes flew wide open, his talons clutched my finger, his ears were depressed, and every motion and look said, "Hands off, at your peril." Finding this game did not work, he soon began to "play 'possum" again. I put a cover over my study wood-box and kept him captive for a week. Look in upon him at any time, night or day, and he was apparently wrapped in the profoundest slumber; but the live mice which I put into his box from time to time found his sleep was easily broken; there would be a sudden rustle in the box, a faint squeak, and then silence. After a week of captivity I gave him his freedom in the full sunshine: no trouble for him to see which way and where to go.

Just at dusk in the winter nights, I often hear his soft *bur-r-r-r*, very pleasing and bell-like. What a furtive, woody sound it is in the winter

stillness, so unlike the harsh scream of the hawk!
But all the ways of the owl are ways of softness
and duskiness. His wings are shod with silence,
his plumage is edged with down.

Another owl neighbor of mine, with whom I pass
the time of day more frequently than with the last,
lives farther away. I pass his castle every night
on my way to the post-office, and in winter, if the
hour is late enough, am pretty sure to see him
standing in his doorway, surveying the passers-by
and the landscape through narrow slits in his eyes.
For four successive winters now have I observed
him. As the twilight begins to deepen, he rises
up out of his cavity in the apple-tree, scarcely
faster than the moon rises from behind the hill,
and sits in the opening, completely framed by its
outlines of gray bark and dead wood, and by his
protective coloring virtually invisible to every eye
that does not know he is there. Probably my own
is the only eye that has ever penetrated his secret,
and mine never would have done so had I not
chanced on one occasion to see him leave his retreat
and make a raid upon a shrike that was impaling
a shrew-mouse upon a thorn in a neighboring tree,
and which I was watching. Failing to get the
mouse, the owl returned swiftly to his cavity, and
ever since, while going that way, I have been on
the lookout for him. Dozens of teams and foot-
passengers pass him late in the day, but he regards
them not, nor they him. When I come along and
pause to salute him, he opens his eyes a little wider,

and, appearing to recognize me, quickly shrinks and
fades into the background of his door in a very
weird and curious manner.   When he is not at his
outlook, or when he is, it requires the best powers
of the eye to decide the point, as the empty cavity
itself is almost an exact image of him.   If the
whole thing had been carefully studied, it could not
have answered its purpose better.   The owl stands
quite perpendicular, presenting a front of light
mottled gray; the eyes are closed to a mere slit,
the ear-feathers depressed, the beak buried in the
plumage, and the whole attitude is one of silent,
motionless waiting and observation.   If a mouse
should be seen crossing the highway, or scudding
over any exposed part of the snowy surface in the
twilight, the owl would doubtless swoop down upon
it.   I think the owl has learned to distinguish me
from the rest of the passers-by; at least, when I
stop before him, and he sees himself observed, he
backs down into his den, as I have said, in a very
amusing manner.   Whether bluebirds, nuthatches,
and chickadees — birds that pass the night in cavities of trees — ever run into the clutches of the
dozing owl, I should be glad to know.   My impression is, however, that they seek out smaller
cavities.   An old willow by the roadside blew down
one summer, and a decayed branch broke open,
revealing a brood of half-fledged owls, and many
feathers and quills of bluebirds, orioles, and other
songsters, showing plainly enough why all birds fear
and berate the owl.

The English house sparrows, which are so rapidly increasing among us, and which must add greatly to the food supply of the owls and other birds of prey, seek to baffle their enemies by roosting in the densest evergreens they can find, in the arbor-vitæ, and in hemlock hedges. Soft-winged as the owl is, he cannot steal in upon such a retreat without giving them warning.

These sparrows are becoming about the most noticeable of my winter neighbors, and a troop of them every morning watch me put out the hens' feed, and soon claim their share. I rather encouraged them in their neighborliness, till one day I discovered the snow under a favorite plum-tree where they most frequently perched covered with the scales of the fruit-buds. On investigating, I found that the tree had been nearly stripped of its buds, — a very unneighborly act on the part of the sparrows, considering, too, all the cracked corn I had scattered for them. So I at once served notice on them that our good understanding was at an end. And a hint is as good as a kick with this bird. The stone I hurled among them, and the one with which I followed them up, may have been taken as a kick; but they were only a hint of the shotgun that stood ready in the corner. The sparrows left in high dudgeon, and were not back again in some days, and were then very shy. No doubt the time is near at hand when we shall have to wage serious war upon these sparrows, as they long have had to do on the continent of Europe. And yet it will be hard to kill the little wretches, the only Old World bird we have. When I take down my gun to shoot them I shall probably remember that the Psalmist said, "I watch, and am as a sparrow alone upon the housetop," and maybe the recollection will cause me to stay my hand. The sparrows have the Old World hardiness and prolificness; they are wise and tenacious of life, and we shall find it by and by no small matter to keep them in check. Our native birds are much different, less prolific, less shrewd, less aggressive and persistent, less quick-witted and able to read the note of danger or hostility, — in short, less sophisticated. Most of our birds are yet essentially wild, that is, little changed by civilization. In winter, especially, they sweep by me and around me in flocks, — the Canada sparrow, the snow bunting, the shore lark, the pine grosbeak, the redpoll, the cedar-bird, — feeding upon frozen apples in the orchard, upon cedar-berries, upon maple-buds, and the berries of the mountain-ash, and the celtis, and upon the seeds of the weeds that rise above the snow in the field, or upon the hayseed dropped where the cattle have been foddered in the barnyard or about the distant stack; but yet taking no heed of man, in no way changing their habits so as to take advantage of his presence in nature. The pine grosbeaks will come in numbers upon your porch to get the black drupes of the honeysuckle or the woodbine, or within reach of your windows to get the berries of the mountain-ash, but they know you not; they look at you as innocently and unconcernedly as at a bear or moose in their native north, and your house is no more to them than a ledge of rocks.

The only ones of my winter neighbors that actually rap at my door are the nuthatches and woodpeckers, and these do not know that it is my door. My retreat is covered with the bark of young chestnut-trees, and the birds, I suspect, mistake it for a huge stump that ought to hold fat grubs (there is not even a book-worm inside of it), and their loud rapping often makes me think I have a caller indeed. I place fragments of hickory-nuts in the interstices of the bark, and thus attract the nuthatches; a bone upon my window-sill attracts both nuthatches and the downy woodpecker. They peep in curiously through the window upon me, pecking away at my bone, too often a very poor one. A bone nailed to a tree a few feet in front of the window attracts crows as well as lesser birds. Even the slate-colored snowbird, a seed-eater, comes and nibbles it occasionally.

The bird that seems to consider he has the best right to the bone both upon the tree and upon the sill is the downy woodpecker, my favorite neighbor among the winter birds, to whom I will mainly devote the remainder of this chapter. His retreat is but a few paces from my own, in the decayed limb of an apple-tree which he excavated several autumns ago. I say "he" because the red plume on the top of his head proclaims the sex. It seems not to be generally known to our writers upon orni-

indifferent, after some delay he shows his head in
his round doorway about ten feet above, and looks
down inquiringly upon me, — sometimes latterly I
think half resentfully, as much as to say, "I would
thank you not to disturb me so often." After sundown, he will not put his head out any more when
I call, but as I step away I can get a glimpse of
him inside looking cold and reserved. He is a late
riser, especially if it is a cold or disagreeable morning, in this respect being like the barn fowls; it is
sometimes near nine o'clock before I see him leave
his tree. On the other hand, he comes home early,
being in, if the day is unpleasant, by four P. M.
He lives all alone; in this respect I do not com-
mend his example. Where his mate is, I should
like to know.

I have discovered several other woodpeckers in
adjoining orchards, each of which has a like home,
and leads a like solitary life. One of them has
excavated a dry limb within easy reach of my hand,
doing the work also in September. But the choice
of tree was not a good one; the limb was too much
decayed, and the workman had made the cavity too
large; a chip had come out, making a hole in the
outer wall. Then he went a few inches down the
limb and began again, and excavated a large, com-
modious chamber, but had again come too near the
surface; scarcely more than the bark protected him
in one place, and the limb was very much weak-
ened. Then he made another attempt still farther
down the limb, and drilled in an inch or two, but

seemed to change his mind; the work stopped, and I concluded the bird had wisely abandoned the tree. Passing there one cold, rainy November day, I thrust in my two fingers and was surprised to feel something soft and warm: as I drew away my hand the bird came out, apparently no more surprised than I was. It had decided, then, to make its home in the old limb; a decision it had occasion to regret, for not long after, on a stormy night, the branch gave way and fell to the ground: —

"When the bough breaks the cradle will fall,
And down will come baby, cradle and all."

Such a cavity makes a snug, warm home, and when the entrance is on the under side of the limb, as is usual, the wind and snow cannot reach the occupant. Late in December, while crossing a high, wooded mountain, lured by the music of fox-hounds, I discovered fresh yellow chips strewing the new-fallen snow, and at once thought of my woodpeckers. On looking around I saw where one had been at work excavating a lodge in a small yellow birch. The orifice was about fifteen feet from the ground, and appeared as round as if struck with a compass. It was on the east side of the tree, so as to avoid the prevailing west and northwest winds. As it was nearly two inches in diameter, it could not have been the work of the downy, but must have been that of the hairy, or else the yellow-bellied woodpecker. His home had probably been wrecked by some violent wind, and he was thus providing himself another. In digging out these retreats the woodpeckers prefer a dry, brittle trunk, not too soft. They go in horizontally to the centre and then turn downward, enlarging the tunnel as they go, till when finished it is the shape of a long, deep pear.

Another trait our woodpeckers have that endears them to me, and that has never been pointedly noticed by our ornithologists, is their habit of drumming in the spring. They are songless birds, and yet all are musicians; they make the dry limbs eloquent of the coming change. Did you think that loud, sonorous hammering which proceeded from the orchard or from the near woods on that still March or April morning was only some bird getting its breakfast? It is downy, but he is not rapping at the door of a grub; he is rapping at the door of spring, and the dry limb thrills beneath the ardor of his blows. Or, later in the season, in the dense forest or by some remote mountain lake, does that measured rhythmic beat that breaks upon the silence, first three strokes following each other rapidly, succeeded by two louder ones with longer intervals between them, and that has an effect upon the alert ear as if the solitude itself had at last found a voice, — does that suggest anything less than a deliberate musical performance? In fact, our woodpeckers are just as characteristically drummers as is the ruffed grouse, and they have their particular limbs and stubs to which they resort for that purpose. Their need of expression is apparently just as great as that of the song-birds, and it

is not surprising that they should have found out
that there is music in a dry, seasoned limb which
can be evoked beneath their beaks.

A few seasons ago, a downy woodpecker, probably the individual one who is now my winter neighbor, began to drum early in March in a partly decayed apple-tree that stands in the edge of a narrow
strip of woodland near me.   When the morning
was still and mild I would often hear him through
my window before I was up, or by half-past six
o'clock, and he would keep it up pretty briskly till
nine or ten o'clock, in this respect resembling the
grouse, which do most of their drumming in the
forenoon.   His drum was the stub of a dry limb
about the size of one's wrist.   The heart was decayed and gone, but the outer shell was hard and
resonant.   The bird would keep his position there
for an hour at a time.   Between his drummings he
would preen his plumage and listen as if for the
response of the female, or for the drum of some
rival.   How swift his head would go when he was
delivering his blows upon the limb! His beak wore
the surface perceptibly.   When he wished to change
the key, which was quite often, he would shift his
position an inch or two to a knot which gave out
a higher, shriller note.   When I climbed up to
examine his drum he was much disturbed.   I did
not know he was in the vicinity, but it seems he
saw me from a near tree, and came in haste to the
neighboring branches, and with spread plumage and
a sharp note demanded plainly enough what my

business was with his drum. I was invading his
privacy, desecrating his shrine, and the bird was
much put out. After some weeks the female appeared; he had literally drummed up a mate; his
urgent and oft-repeated advertisement was answered.
Still the drumming did not cease, but was quite as
fervent as before. If a mate could be won by
drumming, she could be kept and entertained by
more drumming; courtship should not end with
marriage. If the bird felt musical before, of course
he felt much more so now. Besides that, the
gentle deities needed propitiating in behalf of the
nest and young as well as in behalf of the mate.
After a time a second female came, when there was
war between the two. I did not see them come
to blows, but I saw one female pursuing the other
about the place, and giving her no rest for several
days. She was evidently trying to run her out of
the neighborhood. Now and then, she, too, would
drum briefly, as if sending a triumphant message to
her mate.

The woodpeckers do not each have a particular
dry limb to which they resort at all times to drum,
like the one I have described. The woods are full
of suitable branches, and they drum more or less
here and there as they are in quest of food; yet I
am convinced each one has its favorite spot, like
the grouse, to which it resorts especially in the
morning. The sugar-maker in the maple-woods
may notice that this sound proceeds from the same
tree or trees about his camp with great regularity.

A woodpecker in my vicinity has drummed for two seasons on a telegraph pole, and he makes the wires and glass insulators ring. Another drums on a thin board on the end of a long grape-arbor, and on still mornings can be heard a long distance.

A friend of mine in a Southern city tells me of a red-headed woodpecker that drums upon a lightning-rod on his neighbor's house. Nearly every clear, still morning at certain seasons, he says, this musical rapping may be heard. "He alternates his tapping with his stridulous call, and the effect on a cool, autumn-like morning is very pleasing."

The high-hole appears to drum more promiscuously than does downy. He utters his long, loud spring call, *whick — whick — whick — whick*, and then begins to rap with his beak upon his perch before the last note has reached your ear. I have seen him drum sitting upon the ridge of the barn. The log-cock, or pileated woodpecker, the largest and wildest of our Northern species, I have never heard drum. His blows should wake the echoes.

When the woodpecker is searching for food, or laying siege to some hidden grub, the sound of his hammer is dead or muffled, and is heard but a few yards. It is only upon dry, seasoned timber, freed of its bark, that he beats his reveille to spring and wooes his mate.

Wilson was evidently familiar with this vernal drumming of the woodpeckers, but quite misinterprets it. Speaking of the red-bellied species, he says: "It rattles like the rest of the tribe on the

across. They are evidently made to get at the
tender, juicy bark, or cambium layer, next to the
hard wood of the tree. The health and vitality of
the branch are so seriously impaired by them that
it often dies.

In the following winter the same bird (probably)
tapped a maple-tree in front of my window in fifty-
six places; and when the day was sunny, and the
sap oozed out, he spent most of his time there.
He knew the good sap-days, and was on hand
promptly for his tipple; cold and cloudy days he
did not appear. He knew which side of the tree
to tap, too, and avoided the sunless northern expos-
ure. When one series of well-holes failed to supply him, he would sink another, drilling through
the bark with great ease and quickness. Then,
when the day was warm, and the sap ran freely, he
would have a regular sugar-maple debauch, sitting
there by his wells hour after hour, and as fast as
they became filled sipping out the sap. This he
did in a gentle, caressing manner that was very
suggestive. He made a row of wells near the foot
of the tree, and other rows higher up, and he would
hop up and down the trunk as these became filled.
He would hop down the tree backward with the
utmost ease, throwing his tail outward and his head
inward at each hop. When the wells would freeze
up or his thirst become slaked, he would ruffle his
feathers, draw himself together, and sit and doze
in the sun on the side of the tree. He passed the
night in a hole in an apple-tree not far off. He

was evidently a young bird, not yet having the
plumage of the mature male or female, and yet he
knew which tree to tap and where to tap it.   I
saw where he had bored several maples in the
vicinity, but no oaks or chestnuts.   I nailed up a
fat bone near his sap-works: the downy woodpecker
came there several times a day to dine; the nut-
hatch came, and even the snowbird took a taste
occasionally; but this sapsucker never touched it;
the sweet of the tree sufficed for him.   This woodpecker does not breed or abound in my vicinity;
only stray specimens are now and then to be met
with in the colder months.   As spring approached,
the one I refer to took his departure.

I must bring my account of my neighbor in the
tree down to the latest date; so after the lapse of
a year I add the following notes.   The last day of
February was bright and spring-like.   I heard the
first sparrow sing that morning and the first screaming of the circling hawks, and about seven o'clock
the first drumming of my little friend.   His first
notes were uncertain and at long intervals, but by
and by he warmed up and beat a lively tattoo.   As
the season advanced he ceased to lodge in his old
quarters.   I would rap and find nobody at home.
Was he out on a lark, I said, the spring fever
working in his blood?   After a time his drumming
grew less frequent, and finally, in the middle of
April, ceased entirely.   Had some accident befallen
him, or had he wandered away to fresh fields, following some siren of his species?   Probably the

latter. Another bird that I had under observation
also left his winter-quarters in the spring. This,
then, appears to be the usual custom. The wrens
and the nuthatches and chickadees succeed to these
abandoned cavities, and often have amusing disputes
over them. The nuthatches frequently pass the
night in them, and the wrens and chickadees nest
in them. I have further observed that in excavating a cavity for a nest the downy woodpecker
makes the entrance smaller than when he is excavating his winter-quarters. This is doubtless for the
greater safety of the young birds.

The next fall the downy excavated another limb
in the old apple-tree, but had not got his retreat
quite finished when the large hairy woodpecker appeared upon the scene. I heard his loud *click*,
click, early one frosty November morning. There
was something impatient and angry in the tone that
arrested my attention. I saw the bird fly to the
tree where downy had been at work, and fall with
great violence upon the entrance to his cavity.
The bark and the chips flew beneath his vigorous
blows, and, before I fairly woke up to what he was
doing, he had completely demolished the neat, round
doorway of downy. He had made a large, ragged
opening, large enough for himself to enter. I drove
him away and my favorite came back, but only to
survey the ruins of his castle for a moment and
then go away. He lingered about for a day or two
and then disappeared. The big hairy usurper passed
a night in the cavity; but on being hustled out of

it the next night by me, he also left, but not till
he had demolished the entrance to a cavity in a
neighboring tree where downy and his mate had
reared their brood that summer, and where I had
hoped the female would pass the winter.

VIII

WHEN one first catches the smell of the sea, his lungs seem involuntarily to expand, the same as they do when he steps into the open air after long confinement indoors. On the beach he is simply emerging into a larger and more primitive out-of-doors. There before him is aboriginal space, and the breath of it thrills and dilates his body. He stands at the open door of the continent and eagerly drinks the large air. This breeze savors of the original element; it is a breath out of the morning of the world, — bitter, but so fresh and tonic! He has taken salt grossly and at second-hand all his days; now let him inhale it at the fountain-head, and let its impalpable crystals penetrate his spirit, and prick and chafe him into new activity.

We Americans are great eaters of salt, probably the largest eaters of salt and drinkers of water of any of the civilized peoples; the amount of the former consumed annually *per capita* being more than double the amount consumed in England and on the Continent; and the quantity of water (with ice in it) we drink is in still greater proportions. Our dry climate calls for the water, and probably our nervous, dyspeptic tendencies for the salt. Hence our need, as a people, of that great tonic and sedative, the seashore. In Biblical times, new-born babies were rubbed with salt. I suppose it stimulated them and quickened their circulation. American babies are not thus rubbed, and there comes a time with most of us when we feel that the operation cannot be put off any longer, and we rush down to the sea to have the service performed by the old nurse herself, and the pores of both mind and body well cleansed and opened.

Nothing about the sea is more impressive than its ceaseless rocking. Without either wind or tide, it would probably be restless and oscillating, be-cause it registers and passes along the fluctuations of the earthy crust. The solid ground is only rela-tively solid. The scientists, under the direction of the British Association, who sought to determine the influence of the moon upon the earth's crust, found, as soon as their instruments were delicate enough to register the influence of that body, many other agencies at work. They could find no really solid spot to plant their instruments upon. Thus, over the area of a high barometer, the earth's crust bent beneath the weight of the column of air. At sea the waters are pressed down. The waves of the atmospheric ocean, as they sweep around the earth in vast alternations, cause both land and water to rise and fall as beneath the tread of some striding Colossus. This unequal barometric pres-sure over the Atlantic area would, doubtless, of itself keep its equilibrium perpetually disturbed. Thus, "the cradle endlessly rocking," of which our poet sings, is not only bestrode by the winds and swung by the punctual hand of the tides, but the fairest summer weather gives it a nudge, and the bending floor beneath it contributes an impulse. Its rocking is secured beyond peradventure. Darwin seems to think it is the cradle where the primordial life of the globe had its infancy, — a conclusion of science anticipated by an old Greek poet who said, —

"Ocean, father of gods and men."

Whether or not it rocked man, or the germ of man, into being, there can be little doubt that it will continue to rock after he and all things else are wrapped in the final sleep.

Its grandest swing, I found during a couple of weeks' sojourn upon the coast, is often upon a fair day. Local winds and storms make it spiteful and angry. They break up and scatter the waves; but some quiet morning you saunter down to the beach and find the sea beating its long roll. The waves run parallel to the shore and come in with great regularity and deliberation, falling upon it in a succession of long, low cataracts, and you realize the force of the Homeric epithet, "the far-resounding sea." It is a sort of prostrate Niagara expiring in intermittent torrents. Often there is a marked explosion from the compression of the air in the hollow cylinder of the curling wave. These long swells are of the character of those which in the

Hudson follow the passage of one of the great
steamers, — large, measured, uniform.   Something
here has passed, probably a cyclone far at sea; and
these breakers, with their epic swing, are the echo
of its retreating footsteps.

Nothing is more singular and unexpected to
the landsman than the combing of the waves, — a
momentary perpendicular or incurving wall of water,
a few yards from shore, with other water spilling
or pouring over it as over a milldam, thus exhib-
iting for an instant a clear, perfectly-formed cata-
ract.   But instantly the wall crumbles, or is crushed
down, and in place of it there is a wild caldron of
foaming, boiling water and sand.

There seems to be something more cosmic, or shall
I say astronomic, in the sea than in the shore.   Here
you behold the round back of the globe: the lines
are planetary.   You feel that here is the true surface of the sphere, the curving, delicate sides of
this huge bubble.   On the land, amid the wrinkles
of the hills, you have place, fixedness, locality, a
nook in the chimney-corner; but upon the sea you
are literally adrift; place is not, boundaries are not,
space is vacant.   You are upon the smooth disk
of the planet, like a man bestriding the moon.
Under your feet runs the line of the earth's rotund-
ity, and round about you the same curve bounds
your vision.

Then the sea brings us nearer that time when
the earth was without form and void, — a vast,
shoreless, and therefore voiceless, sea.   You look

upon the youth of the world; there is no age, no change, no decay here. It is older than the continents, and, in a measure, their creator. That it should devour them again, like Saturn his children, only adds to our sense of its mystery and power.

The sea is another firmament. The land is fugitive: it abides not. Vast areas have been scalped by the winds and the rains; but the sea, whose law is mutation, changes not, — type of fickleness and instability; yet the granite crumbles, and it remains the same. The semicircle that bounds your view seaward, and that travels with you along the beach, a vast, liquid crescent or half-moon, upon the inner, jagged edge of which you stand, is the type of that which changes not, which neither ends nor begins, and into which all form and all being merge.

This is a part of the vague fascination of the shore; 't is the boundary of two worlds. With your feet upon the present, you confront aboriginal time and space. If we could reach the point in the horizon where the earth and sky meet, we might find the same fascination there. In the absence of this the best substitute is the beach.

We seem to breathe a larger air on the coast. It is the place for large types, large thoughts. 'T is not farms, or a township, we see now, but God's own domain. Possession, ownership, civilization, boundary lines cease, and there within reach is a clear page of terrestrial space, as unmarred and as unmarrable as if plucked from the sidereal heavens.

How inviting and adventurous the ships look,

dropping behind the rim of the horizon, or gently
blown along its edge, their yard-arms pointing to
all quarters of the globe! Mystery, adventure, the
promise of unknown lands, beckon to us from the
full-rigged ships. One does not see them come or
depart; they dawn upon him like his own thoughts,
some dim and shadowy, just hovering on the verge
of consciousness, others white and full, a solace to
the eye. But presently, while you ponder, they
are gone, or else vaguely notch the horizon line.
Illusion, enchantment, hover over the sail-ships.
They have the charm of the ancient world of fable
and romance. They are blown by Homeric winds.
They are a survival from the remotest times. But
yonder comes a black steamship, cutting across this
enchanted circle in defiance of wind and tide; this
is the modern world snubbing and dispelling our
illusions, and putting our poets to flight.

But the veritable oceanic brine there before
one, the continental, primordial, original liquid, the
hoary, eternal sea itself, — what can a lover of
fields and woods make of it? None of the charms
or solacements of birds and flowers here, or of rural
sights and sounds; no repose, no plaintiveness, no
dumb companionship; but a spirit threatening, hun-
gering, remorseless, decoying, fascinating, serpentine, rebelling and forever rebelling against the fiat,
"Thus far shalt thou come, and no farther." The
voice of the sea is unlike any other sound in nature;
more riant and chafing than any roar of woods or
storms. One never ceases to hear the briny, rimy,

weltering quality, — it is salt to the ear no less
than to the smell. One fancies he hears the friction and clashing of the invisible crystals. A
shooting avalanche of snow might have this frosty,
beaded, anfractuous sound. The sands and pebbles
and broken shells have something to do with it;
but without these that threatening, serrated edge
remains, — the grainy, saline voice of the sea.

'T is a pity the fabulous sea-serpent is not a reality. The sea seems to imply such a monster, swimming as a leech swims, with vertical undulations,
splitting the waves, or reposing across them in vast
scaly coils. There is something in the sea that fills
the imagination of men with the image of these
things. The sea-serpent will always be seen by
somebody, because the sea itself is serpentine, —
a writhing, crawling, crested, glistening saurian
with the globe in its embrace. How it rises up
and darts upon you! In storms, its breath blackens
and blights the shore vegetation; it devours the
beach and disgorges it again, and piles the shore
with foam, like masses of unwashed wool. Often
a hissing, sibilant sound seems to issue from under
the edge of the bursting wave. Then that ever-
recurring rustle calls up a vision of some scaly monster uncoiling or measuring its length upon the
sands. I was told of two girls, in bathing-suits,
sitting upon the beach, where the waves, which
were running very high, reached them with only
their laced and embroidered edges; then, as if it
had been getting ready for a spring, a huge wave

rushed up and snatched them both into the sea, and they were drowned. In a few days the body of one was cast up, but the other was never seen again. Such fawning, such treachery, are in the waves.

——The sea shifts its pillow like an uneasy sleeper. The contour of the beach is seldom two days alike; that round, smooth bolster of sand is at times very prominent. The waves stroke and caress it, and slide their delicate sea-draperies over it, as if they were indeed making their bed. When you walk there again it is gone, carried down under the waves, and the beach is low and naked.

Both the sight and the sound of the waves fill the mind with images. One thinks of rockets, windrows, embroideries. How they lift themselves up and grow tall as they approach the shore! They are entering shallower water, they are running aground, and they rise up like vessels.

I saw little in the waves that suggested steeds, but more that reminded of huge sheep. At times they would come wallowing ashore precisely like a great flock or mob of woolly-headed sheep; the wave breaks far out, and then comes that rushing line of tossing, leaping woolly heads and shoulders, diminishing as it comes, and leaving the space behind it strewn with foam. Sometimes the waves look like revolving cylindrical knives, carving the coast. Then they thrust up their thin, crescent-shaped edges, like reapers, reaping only shells and sand; yet one seems to hear the hiss of a great sickle, the crackle of stubble, the rustle of sheaves, and the screening of grain. Then again there is mimic thunder as the waves burst, followed by a sound like the downpouring of torrents of rain. How it shovels the sand and sifts and washes it forever! Every particle of silt goes seaward; it is the earth-pollen with which the sunken floors of the sea are deeply covered. What material for future continents, new worlds and new peoples, is hoarded within its sunless depths! How Darwin longed to read the sealed book of the earth's history that lies buried beneath the sea! He thought it probable that the first continents were there; that the areas of elevation and of subsidence had changed places in the remote past.

Turning over the collections of sea-poetry in the libraries, it is rare enough to find a line or a stanza with the real savor of the shore in it. 'T is mostly fresh-water poetry, very pretty, often spirited and frothy, but seldom gritty, saline, and elemental. That bearded, bristling, savage quality of the sea, to which I have referred, you shall hardly find hinted at, except, perhaps, in Whitman, who is usually ignored in these anthologies. Tennyson's touches, as here and there in "Sea-Dreams," always satisfy, and one chafes that Shakespeare should have left so little on the subject.

The poets make a dead set at the vastness, power, and terror of the sea, and take their fill of these aspects of it. 'T is an easy theme, and soon wearies. We crave the verse that shall give us the taste of the salt spray upon our lips. Bryant's hymn to the sea is noble and stately, but it is only his forest hymn shifted to the shore. It touches the same chords. It has no marine quality or atmosphere. The bitterness and the sweetness of the sea, as of a celestial dragon devouring and purifying, are not in it. The poet wings his lofty flight above sea and shore alike. When Emerson sings of the sea, there is more savor, more tonic air, a closer and stronger hold upon the subject; but even he takes refuge in the vastness of his theme, and speaks through the imperial voice of the sea: —

> "I heard, or seemed to hear, the chiding Sea
> Say, Pilgrim, why so late and slow to come ?
> Am I not always here, thy summer home ?
> Is not my voice thy music, morn and eve,
> My breath thy healthful climate in the heats,
> My touch thy antidote, my bay thy bath ?
> Was ever building like my terraces ?
> Was ever couch magnificent as mine ?"

There are strong lines in Rossetti's "Sea Limits," but, like the others, it is a far-off idealization of the subject, and does not bring one nearer the sea.

There are occasionally good descriptive lines in Miller, as

> " I crossed the hilly sea."

And again, —

> "The ships, black-bellied, climb the sea."

There is something fresh and inviting in this comparison: —

> " As pure as sea-washed sands."

But when the poet of the Sierras places old Neptune on the anxious bench, in this wise, —

> "Behold the ocean on the beach
> Kneel lowly down as if in prayer;
> I hear a moan as of despair,
> While far at sea do toss and reach
> Some things so like white pleading hands,"

one has serious qualms.

The breakers usually suggest to the poets rearing and plunging steeds, as in Arnold: —

> "Now the wild white horses play,
> Champ and chafe and toss in the spray,"

and Stedman's spirited poem, "Surf," makes use of the same image. Byron, in "Childe Harold," lays his hand upon the "mane" of the ocean. Whitman, recalling the shapes and sounds of the shore by moonlight, startles the imagination with this line: —

> "The white arms out in the breakers tirelessly tossing."

One of our poets — Taylor, I think — has applied the epithet "chameleon" to the sea, — "the chameleon sea," — which fits well, for the sea takes on all hues and tints. To the genial Autocrat the sea is "feline" and treacherous, — something of the crouching and leaping tiger in it. The poet of "The New Day," as a foil to his love and admiration for it, calls it "the accursed sea." There is sea-salt in Whitman's poetry, strongly realistic epithets and phrases, that had their birth upon the shore, and that perpetually recur to one as he saunters on the beach. He uses the word "rustling" and the phrase "hoarse and sibilant" to describe the sound of the waves. "The husky-voiced sea" expresses the saline quality to which I have referred: —

"Sea of stretch'd ground-swells,
Sea breathing broad and convulsive breaths,
Sea of the brine of life, and of unshovell'd yet always ready
        graves,
Howler and scooper of storms, capricious and dainty sea,
I am integral with you; I too am of one phase and of all
        phases."
            "Oh, madly the sea pushes upon the land,
                With love, with love."

Or this, written upon the beach at Ocean Grove
in 1883, —

"With husky-haughty lips, O Sea!
Where day and night I wend thy surf-beat shore,
Imaging to my sense thy varied strange suggestions,
The troops of white-maned racers racing to the goal,
Thy ample smiling face, dash'd with the sparkling dimples of
        the sun,
Thy brooding scowl and murk — thy unloos'd hurricanes,
Thy unsubduedness, caprices, wilfulness;
Great as thou art above the rest, thy many tears — a lack from
        all eternity in thy content,
(Naught but the greatest struggles, wrongs, defeats, could make
        thee greatest — no less could make thee,)
Thy lonely state — something thou ever seek'st and seek'st, yet
        never gain'st,
Surely some right withheld — some voice, in huge monotonous
        rage, of freedom-lover pent,
Some vast heart, like a planet's, chain'd and chafing in those
        breakers,
By lengthen'd swell, and spasm, and panting breath,
And rhythmic rasping of thy sands and waves,
And serpent hiss, and savage peals of laughter,
And undertones of distant lion roar,
(Sounding, appealing to the sky's deaf ear — but now, rapport
        for once,
A phantom in the night thy confidant for once,)
The first and last confession of the globe,
Outsurging, muttering from thy soul's abysms,
The tale of cosmic elemental passion,
Thou tellest to a kindred soul."

Whitman is essentially of the shore; his bearded,
aboriginal quality, — something in his words that
smites and chafes, a tonic like salt air, not sweet, but
dilating; his irregular, flowing, repeating, elliptical
lines; his sense of space, and constant reference to
the earth and the orbs as standards and symbols.
His poems are rarely architectural or sculpturesque,
either to the eye or mind; no carving and shaping
for merely art's sake; but floating, drifting, surging
masses of concrete events and images, more or less
nebular, protoplasmic, and preliminary, but always
potent and alive, and full of the salt of the earth,
holding in solution as no other poet does his times
and country.

The sea is the great purifier and equalizer of
climes, the great canceler, leveler, distributer, neu-
tralizer, and sponge of oblivion.   What a cemetery,
and yet what healing in its breath!   What a desert,
and yet what plenty in its depths!   How destructive, and yet the continents are its handiwork.

> "Sea, full of food, the nourisher of kinds,
> Purger of earth, and medicine of men."

And yet famine and thirst, dismay and death,
stalk the wave.   Contradictory, multitudinous sea!
the despoiler and yet the renewer; barren as a rock,
yet as fruitful as a field; old as Time, and young
as to-day; merciless as Fate, and tender as Love;
the fountain of all waters, yet mocking its victims
with the most horrible thirst; smiting like a hammer, and caressing like a lady's palm; falling upon
the shore like a wall of rock, then creeping up the

sands as with the rustle of an infant's drapery; cesspool of the continents, yet "creating a sweet clime by its breath;" pit of terrors, gulf of despair, caldron of hell, yet health, power, beauty, enchantment, dwell forever with the sea.

IX

A SPRING RELISH

IT is a little remarkable how regularly severe and mild winters alternate in our climate for a series of years, — a feminine and a masculine one, as it were, almost invariably following each other. Every other season now for ten years the ice-gatherers on the river have been disappointed of a full harvest, and every other season the ice has formed from fifteen to twenty inches thick. From 1873 to 1884 there was no marked exception to this rule. But in the last-named year, when, according to the succession, a mild winter was due, the breed seemed to have got crossed, and a sort of mongrel winter was the result; neither mild nor severe, but very stormy, capricious, and disagreeable, with ice a foot thick on the river. The winter which followed, that of 1884–85, though slow and hesitating at first, fully proved itself as belonging to the masculine order. The present winter of 1885–86 shows a marked return to the type of two years ago, less hail and snow, but by no means the mild season that was due. By and by, probably, the meteorological influences will get back into the old ruts again, and we shall have once more the regular alternation of mild and severe winters. During very open winters, like that of 1879-80, nature in my latitude, eighty miles north of New York, hardly shuts up house at all. That season I heard a little piping frog on the 7th of December, and on the 18th of January, in a spring run, I saw the common bullfrog out of his hibernaculum, evidently thinking it was spring. A copperhead snake was killed here about the same date; caterpillars did not seem to retire, as they usually do, but came forth every warm day. The note of the bluebird was heard nearly every week all winter, and occasionally that of the robin. Such open winters make one fear that his appetite for spring will be blunted when spring really does come; but he usually finds that the April days have the old relish. April is that part of the season that never cloys upon the palate. It does not surfeit one with good things, but provokes and stimulates the curiosity. One is on the alert, there are hints and suggestions on every hand. Something has just passed, or stirred, or called, or breathed, in the open air or in the ground about, that we would fain know more of. May is sweet, but April is pungent. There is frost enough in it to make it sharp, and heat enough in it to make it quick.

In my walks in April, I am on the lookout for watercresses. It is a plant that has the pungent April flavor. In many parts of the country the watercress seems to have become completely naturalized, and is essentially a wild plant. I found it

one day in a springy place, on the top of a high,
wooded mountain, far from human habitation. We
gathered it and ate it with our sandwiches. Where
the walker cannot find this salad, a good substitute
may be had in our native spring cress, which is also
in perfection in April. Crossing a wooded hill in
the regions of the Catskills on the 15th of the
month, I found a purple variety of the plant, on
the margin of a spring that issued from beneath a
ledge of rocks, just ready to bloom. I gathered
the little white tubers, that are clustered like miniature potatoes at the root, and ate them, and they
were a surprise and a challenge to the tongue; on
the table they would well fill the place of mustard,
and horseradish, and other appetizers. When I
was a schoolboy, we used to gather, in a piece of
woods on our way to school, the roots of a closely
allied species to eat with our lunch. But we generally ate it up before lunch-time. Our name for
this plant was "Crinkle-root." The botanists call
it the toothwort (*Dentaria*), also pepper-root.

From what fact or event shall one really date the
beginning of spring? The little piping frogs usually furnish a good starting-point. One spring I
heard the first note on the 6th of April; the next
on the 27th of February; but in reality the latter
season was only about two weeks earlier than the
former. When the bees carry in their first pollen,
one would think spring had come; yet this fact
does not always correspond with the real stage of
the season. Before there is any bloom anywhere,

bees will bring pollen to the hive.   Where do they
get it?

I have seen them gathering it on the fresh sawdust in the woodyard, especially on that of hickory
or maple.   They wallow amid the dust, working
it over and over, and searching it like diamond-
hunters, and after a time their baskets are filled
with the precious flour, which is probably only a
certain part of the wood, doubtless the soft, nutri-
tious inner bark.

In fact, all signs and phases of life in the early
season are very capricious, and are earlier or later
just as some local or exceptional circumstance favors
or hinders.   It is only such birds as arrive after
about the 20th of April that are at all "punctual"
according to the almanac.   I have never known the
arrival of the barn swallow to vary much from that
date in this latitude, no matter how early or late
the season might be.   Another punctual bird is the
yellow red-poll warbler, the first of his class that
appears.   Year after year, between the 20th and
the 25th, I am sure to see this little bird about my
place for a day or two only, now on the ground,
now on the fences, now on the small trees and
shrubs, and closely examining the buds or just-
opening leaves of the apple-trees.   He is a small
olive-colored bird, with a dark-red or maroon-col-
ored patch on the top of his head.   His ordinary
note is a smart "chirp."   His movements are very
characteristic, especially that vertical, oscillating
movement of the hind part of his body, like that of

the wagtails.   There are many birds that do not
come here till May, be the season never so early.
The spring of 1878 was very forward, and on the
27th of April I made this entry in my note-book:
"In nature it is the middle of May, and, judging
from vegetation alone, one would expect to find
many of the later birds, as the oriole, the wood
thrush, the kingbird, the catbird, the tanager, the
indigo-bird, the vireos, and many of the warblers,
but they have not arrived.   The May birds, it
seems, will not come in April, no matter how the
season favors."

Some birds passing north in the spring are pro-
vokingly silent.   Every April I see the hermit
thrush hopping about the woods, and in case of a
sudden snow-storm seeking shelter about the outbuildings; but I never hear even a fragment of his
wild, silvery strain.   The white-crowned sparrow
also passes in silence.   I see the bird for a few
days about the same date each year, but he will
not reveal to me his song.   On the other hand,
his congener, the white-throated sparrow, is decid-
edly musical in passing, both spring and fall.   His
sweet, wavering whistle is at times quite as full
and perfect as when heard in June or July in the
Canadian woods.   The latter bird is much more
numerous than the white-crowned, and its stay
with us more protracted, which may in a measure
account for the greater frequency of its song.   The
fox sparrow, who passes earlier (sometimes in
March), is also chary of the music with which he

is so richly endowed. It is not every season that
I hear him, though my ear is on the alert for his
strong, finely-modulated whistle.

Nearly all the warblers sing in passing. I hear
them in the orchards, in the groves, in the woods,
as they pause to feed in their northward journey,
their brief, lisping, shuffling, insect-like notes re-
quiring to be searched for by the ear, as their forms
by the eye. But the ear is not tasked to identify
the songs of the kinglets, as they tarry briefly with
us in spring. In fact, there is generally a week
in April or early May, —

> " On such a time as goes before the leaf,
>   When all the woods stand in a mist of green
>   And nothing perfect,"

during which the piping, voluble, rapid, intricate,
and delicious warble of the ruby-crowned kinglet is
the most noticeable strain to be heard, especially
among the evergreens.

I notice that during the mating season of the
birds the rivalries and jealousies are not all confined
to the males. Indeed, the most spiteful and furious
battles, as among the domestic fowls, are frequently
between females. I have seen two hen robins
scratch and pull feathers in a manner that contrasted
strongly with the courtly and dignified sparring
usual between the males. One March a pair of
bluebirds decided to set up housekeeping in the
trunk of an old apple-tree near my house. Not
long after, an unwedded female appeared, and probably tried to supplant the lawful wife. I did not

see what arts she used, but I saw her being very
roughly handled by the jealous bride. The battle
continued nearly all day about the orchard and
grounds, and was a battle at very close quarters.
The two birds would clinch in the air or on a tree,
and fall to the ground with beaks and claws locked.
The male followed them about, and warbled and
called, but whether deprecatingly or encouragingly,
I could not tell. Occasionally, he would take a
hand, but whether to separate them or whether to
fan the flames, that I could not tell. So far as I
could see, he was highly amused, and culpably indifferent to the issue of the battle.

The English spring begins much earlier than
ours in New England and New York, yet an exceptionally early April with us must be nearly, if not
quite, abreast with April as it usually appears in
England. The black-thorn sometimes blooms in
Britain in February, but the swallow does not
appear till about the 20th of April, nor the anemone
bloom ordinarily till that date. The nightingale
comes about the same time, and the cuckoo follows
close. Our cuckoo does not come till near June;
but the water-thrush, which Audubon thought
nearly equal to the nightingale as a songster (though
it certainly is not), I have known to come by the
21st. I have seen the sweet English violet, escaped
from the garden, and growing wild by the roadside,
in bloom on the 25th of March, which is about its
date of flowering at home. During the same season, the first of our native flowers to appear was

the hepatica, which I found on April 4. The arbutus and the dicentra appeared on the 10th, and the coltsfoot — which, however, is an importation — about the same time. The bloodroot, claytonia, saxifrage, and anemone were in bloom on the 17th, and I found the first blue violet and the great spurred violet on the 19th (saw the little violet-colored butterfly dancing about the woods the same day). I plucked my first dandelion on a meadow slope on the 23d, and in the woods, protected by a high ledge, my first trillium. During the month at least twenty native shrubs and wild flowers bloomed in my vicinity, which is an unusual showing for April.

There are many things left for May, but nothing fairer, if as fair, as the first flower, the hepatica. I find I have never admired this little firstling half enough. When at the maturity of its charms, it is certainly the gem of the woods. What an individuality it has! No two clusters alike; all shades and sizes; some are snow-white, some pale pink, with just a tinge of violet, some deep purple, others the purest blue, others blue touched with lilac. A solitary blue-purple one, fully expanded and rising over the brown leaves or the green moss, its cluster of minute anthers showing like a group of pale stars on its little firmament, is enough to arrest and hold the dullest eye. Then, as I have elsewhere stated, there are individual hepaticas, or individual families among them, that are sweet-scented. The gift seems as capricious as the gift of genius in families.

You cannot tell which the fragrant ones are till you try them. Sometimes it is the large white ones, sometimes the large purple ones, sometimes the small pink ones. The odor is faint, and recalls that of the sweet violets. A correspondent, who seems to have carefully observed these fragrant hepaticas, writes me that this gift of odor is constant in the same plant; that the plant which bears sweet-scented flowers this year will bear them next.

There is a brief period in our spring when I like more than at any other time to drive along the country roads, or even to be shot along by steam and have the landscape presented to me like a map. It is at that period, usually late in April, when we behold the first quickening of the earth. The waters have subsided, the roads have become dry, the sunshine has grown strong and its warmth has penetrated the sod; there is a stir of preparation about the farm and all through the country. One does not care to see things very closely; his interest in nature is not special but general. The earth is coming to life again. All the genial and more fertile places in the landscape are brought out; the earth is quickened in spots and streaks; you can see at a glance where man and nature have dealt the most kindly with it. The warm, moist places, the places that have had the wash of some building or of the road, or have been subjected to some special mellowing influence, how quickly the turf awakens there and shows the tender green! See what the

landscape would be, how much earlier spring would
come to it, if every square yard of it was alike
moist and fertile. As the later snows lay in patches
here and there, so now the earliest verdure is irregularly spread over the landscape, and is especially
marked on certain slopes, as if it had blown over
from the other side and lodged there.

A little earlier the homesteads looked cold and
naked; the old farmhouse was bleak and unattrac-
tive; now Nature seems especially to smile upon
it; her genial influences crowd up around it; the
turf awakens all about as if in the spirit of friendli-
ness. See the old barn on the meadow slope; the
green seems to have oozed out from it, and to have
flowed slowly down the hill; at a little distance it
is lost in the sere stubble. One can see where
every spring lies buried about the fields; its influence is felt at the surface, and the turf is early
quickened there. Where the cattle have loved to
lie and ruminate in the warm summer twilight,
there the April sunshine loves to linger too, till the
sod thrills to new life.

The home, the domestic feeling in nature, is
brought out and enhanced at this time; what man
has done tells, especially what he has done well.
Our interest centres in the farmhouses, and in the
influence that seems to radiate from there. The
older the home, the more genial nature looks about
it. The new architectural place of the rich citizen,
with the barns and outbuildings concealed or dis-
guised as much as possible, — spring is in no hurry

about it; the sweat of long years of honest labor
has not yet fattened the soil it stands upon.

The full charm of this April landscape is not
brought out till the afternoon.   It seems to need
the slanting rays of the evening sun to give it the
right mellowness and tenderness, or the right per-
spective.   It is, perhaps, a little too bald in the
strong, white light of the earlier part of the day;
but when the faint, four-o'clock shadows begin to
come out, and we look through the green vistas, and
along the farm lanes toward the west, or out across
long stretches of fields above which spring seems
fairly hovering, just ready to alight, and note the
teams slowly plowing, the brightened mould-board
gleaming in the sun now and then, — it is at such
times we feel its fresh, delicate attraction the most.
There is no foliage on the trees yet; only here and
there the red bloom of the soft maple, illuminated
by the declining sun, shows vividly against the
tender green of a slope beyond, or a willow, like a
thin veil, stands out against a leafless wood.   Here
and there a little meadow watercourse is golden
with marsh marigolds, or some fence border, or
rocky streak of neglected pasture land, is thickly
starred with the white flowers of the bloodroot.
The eye can devour a succession of landscapes at
such a time; there is nothing that sates or entirely
fills it, but every spring token stimulates it and
makes it more on the alert.

April, too, is the time to go budding.   A swell-
ing bud is food for the fancy, and often food for

the eye.   Some buds begin to glow as they begin
to swell.   The bud scales change color and become
a delicate rose pink.   I note this especially in the
European maple.   The bud scales flush as if the
effort to "keep in" brought the blood into their
faces.   The scales of the willow do not flush, but
shine like ebony, and each one presses like a hand
upon the catkin that will escape from beneath it.

When spring pushes pretty hard, many buds
begin to sweat as well as to glow; they exude a
brown, fragrant, gummy substance that affords the
honey-bee her first cement and hive varnish.   The
hickory, the horse-chestnut, the plane-tree, the poplars, are all coated with this April myrrh.   That
of certain poplars, like the Balm of Gilead, is the
most noticeable and fragrant.   No spring incense is
more agreeable.   Its perfume is often upon the
April breeze.   I pick up the bud scales of the poplars along the road, long brown scales like the beaks
of birds, and they leave a rich gummy odor in my
hand that lasts for hours.   I frequently detect the
same odor about my hives when the bees are making all snug against the rains, or against the millers.
When used by the bees, we call it propolis.   Virgil
refers to it as a "glue more adhesive than bird-lime
and the pitch of Phrygian Ida."   Pliny says it is
extracted from the tears of the elm, the willow,
and the reed.   The bees often have serious work to
detach it from their leg-baskets, and make it stick
only where they want it to.

The bud scales begin to drop in April, and by

May Day the scales have fallen from the eyes of
every branch in the forest. In most cases the bud
has an inner wrapping that does not fall so soon.
In the hickory this inner wrapping is like a great
livid membrane, an inch or more in length, thick,
fleshy, and shining. It clasps the tender leaves
about as if both protecting and nursing them. As
the leaves develop, these membranous wrappings
curl back, and finally wither and fall. In the plane-
tree, or sycamore, this inner wrapping of the bud
is a little pelisse of soft yellow or tawny fur.
When it is cast off, it is the size of one's thumb
nail, and suggests the delicate skin of some golden-
haired mole. The young sycamore balls lay aside
their fur wrappings early in May. The flower tas-
sels of the European maple, too, come packed in
a slightly furry covering. The long and fleshy
inner scales that enfold the flowers and leaves are
of a clear olive green, thinly covered with silken
hairs like the young of some animals. Our sugar
maple is less striking and beautiful in the bud, but
the flowers are more graceful and fringe-like.

Some trees have no bud scales. The sumac
presents in early spring a mere fuzzy knot, from
which, by and by, there emerges a soft, furry,
tawny-colored kitten's paw. I know of nothing in
vegetable nature that seems so really to be *born* as
the ferns. They emerge from the ground rolled
up, with a rudimentary and "touch-me-not" look,
and appear to need a maternal tongue to lick them
into shape. The sun plays the wet-nurse to them,

and very soon they are out of that uncanny covering in which they come swathed, and take their
places with other green things.

The bud scales strew the ground in spring as the
leaves do in the fall, though they are so small that
we hardly notice them. All growth, all development, is a casting off, a leaving of something behind.
First the bud scales drop, then the flower drops,
then the fruit drops, then the leaf drops. The
first two are preparatory and stand for spring; the
last two are the crown and stand for autumn.
Nearly the same thing happens with the seed in the
ground. First the shell, or outer husk, is dropped
or cast off; then the cotyledons, those nurse leaves
of the young plant; then the fruit falls, and at last
the stalk and leaf. A bud is a kind of seed planted
in the branch instead of in the soil. It bursts and
grows like a germ. In the absence of seeds and
fruit, many birds and animals feed upon buds.
The pine grosbeaks from the north are the most
destructive budders that come among us. The snow
beneath the maples they frequent is often covered
with bud scales. The ruffed grouse sometimes buds
in an orchard near the woods, and thus takes the
farmer's apple crop a year in advance. Grafting
is but a planting of buds. The seed is a complete, independent bud; it has the nutriment of the
young plant within itself, as the egg holds several
good lunches for the young chick. When the
spider, or the wasp, or the carpenter bee, or the
sand hornet lays an egg in a cell, and deposits food

near it for the young when hatched, it does just
what nature does in every kernel of corn or wheat,
or bean, or nut. Around or within the chit or germ,
she stores food for the young plant. Upon this it
feeds till the root takes hold of the soil and draws
sustenance from thence. The bud is rooted in the
branch, and draws its sustenance from the milk of
the pulpy cambium layer beneath the bark.

Another pleasant feature of spring, which I have
not mentioned, is the full streams. Riding across
the country one bright day in March, I saw and
felt, as if for the first time, what an addition to the
satisfaction one has in the open air at this season are
the clear, full watercourses. They come to the
front, as it were, and lure and hold the eye. There
are no weeds, or grasses, or foliage to hide them;
they are full to the brim, and fuller; they catch
and reflect the sunbeams, and are about the only
objects of life and motion in nature. The trees
stand so still, the fields are so hushed and naked,
the mountains so exposed and rigid, that the eye
falls upon the blue, sparkling, undulating watercourses with a peculiar satisfaction. By and by
the grass and trees will be waving, and the streams
will be shrunken and hidden, and our delight will
not be in them. The still ponds and lakelets will
then please us more.

The little brown brooks, — how swift and full
they ran! One fancied something gleeful and hila-
rious in them. And the large creeks, — how steadily they rolled on, trailing their ample skirts along

the edges of the fields and marshes, and leaving
ragged patches of water here and there! Many a
gentle slope spread, as it were, a turfy apron in
which reposed a little pool or lakelet. Many a
stream sent little detachments across lots, the sparkling water seeming to trip lightly over the unbroken
turf. Here and there an oak or an elm stood
knee-deep in a clear pool, as if rising from its bath.
It gives one a fresh, genial feeling to see such a
bountiful supply of pure, running water. One's
desires and affinities go out toward the full streams.
How many a parched place they reach and lap in
one's memory! How many a vision of naked pebbles and sun-baked banks they cover and blot out!
They give eyes to the fields; they give dimples and
laughter; they give light and motion. _Running
water!_ What a delightful suggestion the words
always convey! One's thoughts and sympathies
are set flowing by them; they unlock a fountain of
pleasant fancies and associations in one's memory;
the imagination is touched and refreshed.

March water is usually clean, sweet water; every
brook is a trout-brook, a mountain brook; the cold
and the snow have supplied the condition of a high
latitude; no stagnation, no corruption, comes downstream now as on a summer freshet. Winter comes
down, liquid and repentant. Indeed, it is more
than water that runs then: it is frost subdued; it
is spring triumphant. No obsolete watercourses
now. The larger creeks seek out their abandoned
beds, return to the haunts of their youth, and lin-

ger fondly there. The muskrat is adrift, but not homeless; his range is vastly extended, and he evidently rejoices in full streams. Through the tunnel of the meadow - mouse the water rushes as through a pipe; and that nest of his, that was so warm and cozy beneath the snowbank in the meadow-bottom, is sodden or afloat. But meadow-mice are not afraid of water. On various occasions I have seen them swimming about the spring pools like muskrats, and, when alarmed, diving beneath the water. Add the golden willows to the full streams, with the red-shouldered starlings perched amid their branches, sending forth their strong, liquid, gurgling notes, and the picture is complete. The willow branches appear to have taken on a deeper yellow in spring; perhaps it is the effect of the stronger sunshine, perhaps it is the effect of the swift vital water laving their roots. The epaulettes of the starlings, too, are brighter than when they left us in the fall, and they appear to get brighter daily until the nesting begins. The males arrive many days before the females, and, perched along the marshes and watercourses, send forth their liquid, musical notes, passing the call from one to the other, as if to guide and hurry their mates forward.

The noise of a brook, you may observe, is by no means in proportion to its volume. The full March streams make far less noise relatively to their size than the shallower streams of summer, because the rocks and pebbles that cause the sound in summer are deeply buried beneath the current. "Still

waters run deep" is not so true as "deep waters
run still." I rode for half a day along the upper
Delaware, and my thoughts almost unconsciously
faced toward the full, clear river. Both the Delaware and the Susquehanna have a starved, impov-
erished look in summer, — unsightly stretches of
naked drift and bare, bleaching rocks. But behold
them in March, after the frost has turned over to
them the moisture it has held back and stored up
as the primitive forests used to hold the summer
rains. Then they have an easy, ample, triumphant
look, that is a feast to the eye. A plump, well-fed
stream is as satisfying to behold as a well-fed animal or a thrifty tree. One source of charm in the
English landscape is the full, placid stream the season through; no desiccated watercourses will you
see there, nor any feeble, decrepit brooks, hardly
able to get over the ground.

This condition of our streams and rivers in
spring is evidently but a faint reminiscence of their
condition during what we may call the geological
springtime, the March or April of the earth's history, when the annual rainfall appears to have
been vastly greater than at present, and when the
watercourses were consequently vastly larger and
fuller. In pleistocene days the earth's climate was
evidently much damper than at present. It was
the rainiest of March weather. On no other theory
can we account for the enormous erosion of the
earth's surface, and the plowing of the great valleys. Professor Newberry finds abundant evidence
that the Hudson was, in former times, a much

larger river than now. Professor Zittel reaches the
same conclusion concerning the Nile, and Humboldt
was impressed with the same fact while examining
the Orinoco and the tributaries of the Amazon. All
these rivers appear to be but mere fractions of their
former selves. The same is true of all the great
lakes. If not Noah's flood, then evidently some
other very wet spell, of which this is a tradition,
lies far behind us. Something like the drought of
summer is beginning upon the earth; the great
floods have dried up; the rivers are slowly shrink-
ing; the water is penetrating farther and farther
into the cooling crust of the earth; and what was
ample to drench and cover its surface, even to make
a Noah's flood, will be but a drop in the bucket to
the vast interior of the cooled sphere.

X

A RIVER VIEW

A SMALL river or stream flowing by one's door
has many attractions over a large body of
water like the Hudson. One can make a companion of it; he can walk with it and sit with it, or
lounge on its banks, and feel that it is all his own.
It becomes something private and special to him.
You cannot have the same kind of attachment and
sympathy with a great river; it does not flow
through your affections like a lesser stream. The
Hudson is a long arm of the sea, and it has something of the sea's austerity and grandeur. I think
one might spend a lifetime upon its banks without feeling any sense of ownership in it, or becoming
at all intimate with it: it keeps one at arm's length.
It is a great highway of travel and of commerce;
ships from all parts of our seaboard plow its waters.

But there is one thing a large river does for
one that is beyond the scope of the companionable
streams, — it idealizes the landscape, it multiplies
and heightens the beauty of the day and of the season. A fair day it makes more fair, and a wild
and tempestuous day it makes more wild and tempestuous. It takes on so quickly and completely

the mood and temper of the sky above. The storm
is mirrored in it, and the wind chafes it into foam.
The face of winter it makes doubly rigid and corpse-
like. How stark and still and white it lies there!
But of a bright day in spring, what life and light
possess it! How it enhances or emphasizes the
beauty of those calm, motionless days of summer
or fall, — the broad, glassy surface perfectly dupli-
cating the opposite shore, sometimes so smooth that
the finer floating matter here and there looks like
dust upon a mirror; the becalmed sails standing
this way and that, drifting with the tide. Indeed,
nothing points a calm day like a great motionless
sail; it is such a conspicuous bid for the breeze
which comes not.

I have observed that when the river is roily, the
fact is not noticeable on a calm day; a glassy surface is a kind of mask. But when the breeze comes
and agitates it a little, its real color comes out.

"Immortal water," says Thoreau, "alive to the
superficies." How sensitive and tremulous and
palpitating this great river is! It is only in certain lights, on certain days, that we can see how it
quivers and throbs. Sometimes you can see the
subtle tremor or impulse that travels in advance of
the coming steamer and prophesies of its coming.
Sometimes the coming of the flood-tide is heralded
in the same way. Always, when the surface is
calm enough and the light is favorable, the river
seems shot through and through with tremblings
and premonitions.

The river never seems so much a thing of life
as in the spring when it first slips off its icy fet-
ters. The dead comes to life before one's very eyes.
The rigid, pallid river is resurrected in a twinkling.
You look out of your window one moment, and
there is that great, white, motionless expanse; you
look again, and there in its place is the tender,
dimpling, sparkling water. But if your eyes are
sharp, you may have noticed the signs all the forenoon; the time was ripe, the river stirred a little in
its icy shroud, put forth a little streak or filament
of blue water near shore, made breathing-holes.
Then, after a while, the ice was rent in places, and
the edges crushed together or shoved one slightly
upon the other; there was apparently something
growing more and more alive and restless under-
neath. Then suddenly the whole mass of the ice
from shore to shore begins to move downstream, —
very gently, almost imperceptibly at first, then with
a steady, deliberate pace that soon lays bare a large
expanse of bright, dancing water. The island above
keeps back the northern ice, and the ebb tide makes
a clean sweep from that point south for a few
miles, until the return of the flood, when the ice
comes back.

After the ice is once in motion, a few hours suf-
fice to break it up pretty thoroughly. Then what
a wild, chaotic scene the river presents: in one part
of the day the great masses hurrying downstream,
crowding and jostling each other, and struggling for
the right of way; in the other, all running up-

stream again, as if sure of escape in that direction.
Thus they race up and down, the sport of the ebb
and flow; but the ebb wins each time by some distance.   Large fields from above, where the men
were at work but a day or two since, come down;
there is their pond yet clearly defined and full of
marked ice; yonder is a section of their canal
partly filled with the square blocks on their way
to the elevators; a piece of a race-course, or a part
of a road where teams crossed, comes drifting by.
The people up above have written their winter
pleasure and occupations upon this page, and we
read the signs as the tide bears it slowly past.
Some calm, bright days the scattered and dimin-
ished masses glide by like white clouds across an
April sky.

At other times, when the water is black and still,
the river looks like a strip of the firmament at
night, dotted with stars and moons in the shape of
little and big fragments of ice.   One day, I remember, there came gliding into my vision a great irregular hemisphere of ice, that vividly suggested the
half moon under the telescope; its white uneven
surface, pitted and cracked, the jagged inner line,
the outward curve, but little broken, and the blue-
black surface upon which it lay, all recalled the
scenery of the midnight skies.   It is only in exceptionally calm weather that the ice collects in these
vast masses, leaving broad expanses of water perfectly clear.   Sometimes, during such weather, it
drifts by in forms that suggest the great continents,

as they appear upon the map, surrounded by the oceans, all their capes and peninsulas, and isthmuses and gulfs, and inland lakes and seas, vividly reproduced.

If the opening of the river is gentle, the closing of it is sometimes attended by scenes exactly the reverse.

A cold wave one December was accompanied by a violent wind, which blew for two days and two nights. The ice formed rapidly in the river, but the wind and waves kept it from uniting and massing. On the second day the scene was indescribably wild and forbidding; the frost and fury of December were never more vividly pictured: vast crumpled, spumy ice-fields interspersed with stretches of wildly agitated water, the heaving waves thick with forming crystals, the shores piled with frozen foam and pulverized floes. After the cold wave had spent itself and the masses had become united and stationary, the scene was scarcely less wild. I fancied the plain looked more like a field of lava and scoria than like a field of ice, an eruption from some huge frost volcano of the north. Or did it suggest that a battle had been fought there, and that this wild confusion was the ruin wrought by the contending forces?

No sooner has the river pulled his icy coverlid over him than he begins to snore in his winter sleep. It is a singular sound. Thoreau calls it a "whoop," Emerson a "cannonade," and in "Merlin" speaks of

"the gasp and moan
Of the ice-imprisoned flood."

Sometimes it is a well-defined grunt, — *e-h-h,* *e-h-h,*
as if some ice-god turned uneasily in his bed.

One fancies the sound is like this, when he hears
it in the still winter nights seated by his fireside, or
else when snugly wrapped in his own bed.

One winter the river shut up in a single night,
beneath a cold wave of great severity and extent.
Zero weather continued nearly a week, with a clear
sky and calm, motionless air; and the effect of the
brilliant sun by day and of the naked skies by
night upon this vast area of new black ice, one expanding it, the other contracting, was very marked.

A cannonade indeed! As the morning advanced,
out of the sunshine came peal upon peal of soft
mimic thunder; occasionally becoming a regular
crash, as if all the ice batteries were discharged at
once. As noon approached, the sound grew to one
continuous mellow roar, which lessened and became
more intermittent as the day waned, until about
sundown it was nearly hushed. Then, as the chill
of night came on, the conditions were reversed, and
the ice began to thunder under the effects of con-
traction; cracks opened from shore to shore, and
grew to be two or three inches broad under the
shrinkage of the ice. On the morrow the expansion
of the ice often found vent in one of these cracks;
the two edges would first crush together, and then
gradually overlap each other for two feet or more.

This expansive force of the sun upon the ice is

sometimes enormous. I have seen the ice explode with a loud noise and a great commotion in the water, and a huge crack shoot like a thunderbolt from shore to shore, with its edges overlapping and shivered into fragments.

When unprotected by a covering of snow, the ice, under the expansive force of the sun, breaks regularly, every two or three miles, from shore to shore.   The break appears as a slight ridge, formed by the edges of the overlapping ice.

This icy uproar is like thunder, because it seems to proceed from something in swift motion; you cannot locate it; it is everywhere and yet nowhere. There is something strange and phantom-like about it.   To the eye all is still and rigid, but to the ear all is in swift motion.

This crystal cloud does not open and let the bolt leap forth, but walk upon it and you see the ice shot through and through in every direction with shining, iridescent lines where the force passed. These lines are not cracks which come to the surface, but spiral paths through the ice, as if the force that made them went with a twist like a rifle bullet. In places several of them run together, when they make a track as broad as one's hand.

Sometimes, when I am walking upon the ice and this sound flashes by me, I fancy it is like the stroke of a gigantic skater, one who covers a mile at a stride and makes the crystal floor ring beneath him.   I hear his long tapering stroke ring out just beside me, and then in a twinkling it is half a mile away.

A fall of snow, and this icy uproar is instantly hushed, the river sleeps in peace. The snow is like a coverlid, which protects the ice from the changes of temperature of the air, and brings repose to its uneasy spirit.

A dweller upon its banks, I am an interested spectator of the spring and winter harvests which its waters yield. In the stern winter nights, it is a pleasant thought that a harvest is growing down there on those desolate plains which will bring work to many needy hands by and by, and health and comfort to the great cities some months later. When the nights are coldest, the ice grows as fast as corn in July. It is a crop that usually takes two or three weeks to grow, and, if the water is very roily or brackish, even longer. Men go out from time to time and examine it, as the farmer goes out and examines his grain or grass, to see when it will do to cut. If there comes a deep fall of snow before the ice has attained much thickness, it is "pricked," so as to let the water up through and form snow-ice. A band of fifteen or twenty men, about a yard apart, each armed with a chisel-bar and marching in line, puncture the ice at each step with a single sharp thrust. To and fro they go, leaving a belt behind them that presently becomes saturated with water. But ice, to be first quality, must grow from beneath, not from above. It is a crop quite as uncertain as any other. A good yield every two or three years, as they say of wheat out West, is about all that can be counted upon. When

there is an abundant harvest, after the ice-houses
are filled, they stack great quantities of it, as the
farmer stacks his surplus hay.

The cutting and gathering of the ice enlivens
these broad, white, desolate fields amazingly. One
looks down upon the busy scene as from a hill-
top upon a river meadow in haying time, only here
the figures stand out much more sharply than they
do from a summer meadow. There is the broad,
straight, blue-black canal emerging into view, and
running nearly across the river; this is the highway
that lays open the farm. On either side lie the
fields or ice-meadows, each marked out by cedar or
hemlock boughs. The farther one is cut first, and,
when cleared, shows a large, long, black parallelo-
gram in the midst of the plain of snow. Then the
next one is cut, leaving a strip or tongue of ice
between the two for the horses to move and turn
upon. Sometimes nearly two hundred men and
boys, with numerous horses, are at work at once,
marking, plowing, planing, scraping, sawing, hauling, chiseling; some floating down the pond on
great square islands towed by a horse, or their fel-
low-workmen; others distributed along the canal,
bending to their ice-hooks; others upon the bridges,
separating the blocks with their chisel-bars; others
feeding the elevators; while knots and straggling
lines of idlers here and there look on in cold discon-
tent, unable to get a job.

The best crop of ice is an early crop. Late in
the season, or after January, the ice is apt to get

"sunstruck," when it becomes "shaky," like a piece
of poor timber. The sun, when he sets about
destroying the ice, does not simply melt it from the
surface, — that were a slow process; but he sends
his shafts into it and separates it into spikes and
needles, — in short, makes kindling-wood of it, so
as to consume it the quicker.

One of the prettiest sights about the ice-harvest-
ing is the elevator in operation. When all works
well, there is an unbroken procession of the great
crystal blocks slowly ascending this incline. They
go up in couples, arm in arm, as it were, like
friends up a stairway, glowing and changing in the
sun, and recalling the precious stones that adorned
the walls of the celestial city. When they reach
the platform where they leave the elevator, they
seem to step off like things of life and volition;
they are still in pairs, and separate only as they
enter upon the "runs." But here they have an
ordeal to pass through, for they are subjected to
a rapid inspection by a man with a sharp eye in his
head and a sharp ice-hook in his hand, and the
black sheep are separated from the flock; every
square with a trace of sediment or earth-stain in it,
whose texture is not the perfect and unclouded crystal, is rejected, and sent hurling down into the
abyss. Those that pass the examination glide into
the building along the gentle incline, and are
switched off here and there upon branch runs, and
distributed to all parts of the immense interior.
When the momentum becomes too great, the blocks

run over a board full of nails or spikes, that scratch
their bottoms and retard their progress, giving the
looker-on an uncomfortable feeling.

A beautiful phenomenon may at times be witnessed on the river in the morning after a night of
extreme cold.   The new black ice is found to be
covered with a sudden growth of frost ferns, — exquisite fern-like formations from a half inch to an
inch in length, standing singly and in clusters, and
under the morning sun presenting a most novel
appearance.   They impede the skate, and are presently broken down and blown about by the wind.

The scenes and doings of summer are counter-
feited in other particulars upon these crystal plains.
Some bright, breezy day you casually glance down
the river and behold a sail, — a sail like that of a
pleasure yacht of summer.   Is the river open again
below there? is your first half-defined inquiry.   But
with what unwonted speed the sail is moving across
the view!   Before you have fairly drawn another
breath it has turned, unperceived, and is shooting with equal swiftness in the opposite direction.
Who ever saw such a lively sail!   It does not bend
before the breeze, but darts to and fro as if it
moved in a vacuum, or like a shadow over a screen.
Then you remember the ice-boats, and you open
your eyes to the fact.   Another and another come
into view around the elbow, turning and flashing
in the sun, and hurtling across each other's path
like white-winged gulls.   They turn so quickly, and
dash off again at such speed, that they produce the

illusion of something singularly light and intan-
gible. In fact, an ice-boat is a sort of disembodied
yacht; it is a sail on skates. The only semblance
to a boat is the sail and the rudder. The platform
under which the skates or runners — three in number — are rigged is broad and low; upon this the
pleasure-seekers, wrapped in their furs or blankets,
lie at full length, and, looking under the sail, skim
the frozen surface with their eyes. The speed
attained is sometimes very great, — more than a
mile per minute, and sufficient to carry them ahead
of the fastest express train. When going at this
rate the boat will leap like a greyhound, and thrilling stories are told of the fearful crevasses, or open
places in the ice, that are cleared at a bound. And
yet withal she can be brought up to the wind so
suddenly as to shoot the unwary occupants off, and
send them skating on their noses some yards.

Navigation on the Hudson stops about the last
of November. There is usually more or less floating ice by that time, and the river may close very
abruptly. Beside that, new ice an inch or two
thick is the most dangerous of all; it will cut
through a vessel's hull like a knife. In 1875 there
was a sudden fall of the mercury the 28th of November. The hard and merciless cold came down
upon the naked earth with great intensity. On the
29th the ground was a rock, and, after the sun went
down, the sky all around the horizon looked like
a wall of chilled iron. The river was quickly covered with great floating fields of smooth, thin ice.

About three o'clock the next morning — the mercury two degrees below zero — the silence of our part of the river was suddenly broken by the alarm bell of a passing steamer; she was in the jaws of the icy legions, and was crying for help; many sleepers alongshore remembered next day that the sound of a bell had floated across their dreams, without arousing them. One man was awakened before long by a loud pounding at his door. On opening it, a tall form, wet and icy, fell in upon him with the cry, "The Sunnyside is sunk!" The man proved to be one of her officers, and was in quest of help. He had made his way up a long hill through the darkness, his wet clothes freezing upon him, and his strength gave way the moment succor was found. Other dwellers in the vicinity were aroused, and with their boats rendered all the assistance possible. The steamer sank but a few yards from shore, only a part of her upper deck remaining above water, yet a panic among the passengers — the men behaving very badly — swamped the boats as they were being filled with the women, and a dozen or more persons were drowned.

When the river is at its wildest, usually in March, the eagles appear. They prowl about amid the ice-floes, alighting upon them or flying heavily above them in quest of fish, or a wounded duck or other game.

I have counted ten of these noble birds at one time, some seated grim and motionless upon cakes of ice, — usually surrounded by crows, — others flap-

ping along, sharply scrutinizing the surface beneath.
Where the eagles are, there the crows do congregate.
The crow follows the eagle, as the jackal follows
the lion, in hope of getting the leavings of the royal
table. Then I suspect the crow is a real hero-wor-
shiper. I have seen a dozen or more of them sitting in a circle about an eagle upon the ice, all with
their faces turned toward him, and apparently in
silent admiration of the dusky king.

The eagle seldom or never turns his back upon
a storm. I think he loves to face the wildest elemental commotion. I shall long carry the picture
of one I saw floating northward on a large raft of
ice one day, in the face of a furious gale of snow.
He stood with his talons buried in the ice, his head
straight out before him, his closed wings showing
their strong elbows, — a type of stern defiance and
power.

This great metropolitan river, as it were, with
its floating palaces, and shores lined with villas, is
thus an inlet and a highway of the wild and the
savage. The wild ducks and geese still follow it
north in spring, and south in the fall. The loon
pauses in his migrations and disports himself in its
waters. Seals and otters are occasionally seen in it.

Of the Hudson it may be said that it is a very
large river for its size, — that is, for the quantity
of water it discharges into the sea. Its water-shed
is comparatively small, — less, I think, than that of
the Connecticut.

It is a huge trough with a very slight incline,

through which the current moves very slowly, and
which would fill from the sea were its supplies from
the mountains cut off. Its fall from Albany to the
bay is only about five feet. Any object upon it,
drifting with the current, progresses southward no
more than eight miles in twenty-four hours. The
ebb tide will carry it about twelve miles, and the
flood set it back from seven to nine. A drop of
water at Albany, therefore, will be nearly three
weeks in reaching New York, though it will get
pretty well pickled some days earlier.

Some rivers by their volume and impetuosity
penetrate the sea, but here the sea is the aggressor,
and sometimes meets the mountain water nearly
half way.

This fact was illustrated a few years ago, when
the basin of the Hudson was visited by one of the
most severe droughts ever known in this part of the
State. In the early winter, after the river was
frozen over above Poughkeepsie, it was discovered
that immense numbers of fish were retreating upstream before the slow encroachment of the salt
water. There was a general exodus of the finny
tribes from the whole lower part of the river; it
was like the spring and fall migration of the birds,
or the fleeing of the population of a district before
some approaching danger: vast swarms of catfish,
white and yellow perch, and striped bass were *en
route* for the fresh water farther north. When the
people alongshore made the discovery, they turned
out as they do in the rural districts when the

pigeons appear, and, with small gillnets let down through holes in the ice, captured them in fabulous numbers. On the heels of the retreating perch and catfish came the denizens of salt water, and codfish were taken ninety miles above New York. When the February thaw came, and brought up the volume of fresh water again, the sea brine was beaten back, and the fish, what were left of them, resumed their old feeding-grounds.

It is this character of the Hudson, this encroachment of the sea upon it, that has led Professor Newberry to speak of it as a drowned river. We have heard of drowned lands, but here is a river overflowed and submerged in the same manner. It is quite certain, however, that this has not always been the character of the Hudson. Its great trough bears evidence of having been worn to its present dimensions by much swifter and stronger currents than those that course through it now. Hence Professor Newberry has advanced the bold and striking theory that in pre-glacial times this part of the continent was several hundred feet higher than at present, and that the Hudson was then a very large and rapid stream, that drew its main supplies from the basin of the Great Lakes through an ancient river-bed that followed pretty nearly the line of the present Mohawk; in other words, that the waters of the St. Lawrence once found an outlet through this channel, debouching into the ocean from a broad, littoral plain, at a point eighty miles southeast of New York, where the sea now rolls

five hundred feet deep. According to the sound-
ings of the coast survey, this ancient bed of the
Hudson is distinctly marked upon the ocean floor
to the point indicated.

To the gradual subsidence of this part of the
continent, in connection with the great changes
wrought by the huge glacier that crept down from
the north during what is called the ice period, is
owing the character and aspects of the Hudson as
we see and know them. The Mohawk valley was
filled up by the drift, and the pent-up waters of
the Great Lakes found an opening through what is
now the St. Lawrence. The trough of the Hudson
was also partially filled, and has remained so to the
present day. There is, perhaps, no point in the
river where the mud and clay are not from two to
three times as deep as the water.

That ancient and grander Hudson lies back of us
several hundred thousand years, — perhaps more,
for a million years are but as one tick of the time-
piece of the Lord; yet even *it* was a juvenile compared with some of the rocks and mountains the
Hudson of to-day mirrors. The Highlands date
from the earliest geological age, — the primary; the
river — the old river — from the latest, the ter-
tiary; and what that difference means in terrestrial
years hath not entered into the mind of man to
conceive. Yet how the venerable mountains open
their ranks for the stripling to pass through. Of
course the river did not force its way through this
barrier, but has doubtless found an opening there

of which it has availed itself, and which it has
enlarged.

In thinking of these things, one only has to allow
time enough, and the most stupendous changes in
the topography of the country are as easy and natural as the going out or the coming in of spring or
summer. According to the authority above referred
to, that part of our coast that flanks the mouth of
the Hudson is still sinking at the rate of a few
inches per century, so that in the twinkling of a
hundred thousand years or so the sea will completely submerge the city of New York, the top of
Trinity Church steeple alone standing above the
flood. We who live so far inland, and sigh for the
salt water, need only to have a little patience, and
we shall wake up some fine morning and find the
surf beating upon our doorsteps.

XI

BIRD ENEMIES

HOW surely the birds know their enemies!
See how the wrens and robins and bluebirds
pursue and scold the cat, while they take little or
no notice of the dog! Even the swallow will fight
the cat, and, relying too confidently upon its powers of flight, sometimes swoops down so near to its
enemy that it is caught by a sudden stroke of the
cat's paw. The only case I know of in which our
small birds fail to recognize their enemy is furnished
by the shrike; apparently the little birds do not
know that this modest-colored bird is an assassin.
At least I have never seen them scold or molest
him, or utter any outcries at his presence, as they
usually do at birds of prey. Probably it is because
the shrike is a rare visitant, and is not found in this
part of the country during the nesting season of our
songsters.

But the birds have nearly all found out the trick
of the jay, and, when he comes sneaking through
the trees in May and June in quest of eggs, he is
quickly exposed and roundly abused. It is amusing to see the robins bustle him out of the tree
which holds their nest. They cry, "Thief, thief!"

to the top of their voices as they charge upon him, and the jay retorts in a voice scarcely less complimentary as he makes off.

The jays have their enemies also, and need to keep an eye on their own eggs. It would be interesting to know if jays ever rob jays, or crows plunder crows; or is there honor among thieves even in the feathered tribes? I suspect the jay is often punished by birds which are otherwise innocent of nest-robbing. One season I found a jay's nest in a small cedar on the side of a wooded ridge. It held five eggs, every one of which had been punctured. Apparently some bird had driven its sharp beak through their shells, with the sole intention of destroying them, for no part of the contents of the eggs had been removed. It looked like a case of revenge; as if some thrush or warbler, whose nest had suffered at the hands of the jays, had watched its opportunity and had in this way retaliated upon its enemies. An egg for an egg. The jays were lingering near, very demure and silent, and probably ready to join a crusade against nest-robbers.

The great bugaboo of the birds is the owl. The owl snatches them from off their roosts at night, and gobbles up their eggs and young in their nests. He is a veritable ogre to them, and his presence fills them with consternation and alarm.

One season, to protect my early cherries, I placed a large stuffed owl amid the branches of the tree. Such a racket as there instantly began about my grounds is not pleasant to think upon! The orioles

and robins fairly "shrieked out their affright."
The news instantly spread in every direction, and
apparently every bird in town came to see that owl
in the cherry-tree, and every bird took a cherry, so
that I lost more fruit than if I had left the owl
indoors. With craning necks and horrified looks
the birds alighted upon the branches, and between
their screams would snatch off a cherry, as if the
act was some relief to their outraged feelings.

The chirp and chatter of the young of birds
which build in concealed or inclosed places, like
the woodpeckers, the house wren, the high-hole,
the oriole, etc., is in marked contrast to the silence
of the fledgelings of most birds that build open and
exposed nests. The young of the sparrows, — unless the social sparrow be an exception, — warblers,
flycatchers, thrushes, etc., never allow a sound to
escape them and, on the alarm note of their parents
being heard, sit especially close and motionless,
while the young of chimney swallows, woodpeckers,
and oriole are very noisy. The latter, in their deep
pouch, are quite safe from birds of prey, except perhaps the owl. The owl, I suspect, thrusts its leg
into the cavities of woodpeckers and into the pocket-
like nest of the oriole, and clutches and brings forth
the birds in its talons. In one case which I heard
of, a screech owl had thrust its claw into a cavity
in a tree, and grasped the head of a red-headed
woodpecker; being apparently unable to draw its
prey forth, it had thrust its own round head into
the hole, and in some way became fixed there, and
had thus died with the woodpecker in its talons.

The life of birds is beset with dangers and mishaps of which we know little. One day, in my walk, I came upon a goldfinch with the tip of one wing securely fastened to the feathers of its rump by what appeared to be the silk of some caterpillar. The bird, though uninjured, was completely crippled, and could not fly a stroke. Its little body was hot and panting in my hands, as I carefully broke the fetter. Then it darted swiftly away with a happy cry. A record of all the accidents and tragedies of bird life for a single season would show many curious incidents. A friend of mine opened his box stove one fall to kindle a fire in it, when he beheld in the black interior the desiccated forms of two bluebirds. The birds had probably taken refuge in the chimney during some cold spring storm, and had come down the pipe to the stove, from whence they were unable to ascend. A peculiarly touching little incident of bird life occurred to a caged female canary. Though unmated, it laid some eggs, and the happy bird was so carried away by her feelings that she would offer food to the eggs, and chatter and twitter, trying, as it seemed, to encourage them to eat! The incident is hardly tragic, neither is it comic.

Certain birds nest in the vicinity of our houses and outbuildings, or even in and upon them, for protection from their enemies, but they often thus expose themselves to a plague of the most deadly character.

I refer to the vermin with which their nests

often swarm, and which kill the young before they
are fledged. In a state of nature this probably
never happens; at least I have never seen or heard
of it happening to nests placed in trees or under
rocks. It is the curse of civilization falling upon
the birds which come too near man. The vermin,
or the germ of the vermin, is probably conveyed to
the nest in hen's feathers, or in straws and hairs
picked up about the barn or hen-house. A robin's
nest upon your porch or in your summer-house will
occasionally become an intolerable nuisance from
the swarms upon swarms of minute vermin with
which it is filled. The parent birds stem the tide
as long as they can, but are often compelled to leave
the young to their terrible fate.

One season a phœbe-bird built on a projecting
stone under the eaves of the house, and all appeared
to go well till the young were nearly fledged, when
the nest suddenly became a bit of purgatory. The
birds kept their places in their burning bed till they
could hold out no longer, when they leaped forth
and fell dead upon the ground.

After a delay of a week or more, during which
I imagine the parent birds purified themselves by
every means known to them, the couple built another nest a few yards from the first, and proceeded
to rear a second brood; but the new nest developed
into the same bed of torment that the first did, and
the three young birds, nearly ready to fly, perished
as they sat within it. The parent birds then left
the place as if it had been accursed.

I imagine the smaller birds have an enemy in
our native white-footed mouse, though I have not
proof enough to convict him. But one season the
nest of a chickadee which I was observing was
broken up in a position where nothing but a mouse
could have reached it. The bird had chosen a
cavity in the limb of an apple-tree which stood but
a few yards from the house. The cavity was deep,
and the entrance to it, which was ten feet from the
ground, was small. Barely light enough was ad-
mitted, when the sun was in the most favorable
position, to enable one to make out the number of
eggs, which was six, at the bottom of the dim interior. While one was peering in and trying to get
his head out of his own light, the bird would star-
tle him by a queer kind of puffing sound. She
would not leave her nest like most birds, but really
tried to blow, or scare, the intruder away; and
after repeated experiments I could hardly refrain
from jerking my head back when that little explosion of sound came up from the dark interior. One
night, when incubation was about half finished, the
nest was harried. A slight trace of hair or fur at
the entrance led me to infer that some small animal
was the robber. A weasel might have done it, as
they sometimes climb trees, but I doubt if either
a squirrel or a rat could have passed the entrance.

Probably few persons have ever suspected the catbird of being an egg-sucker; I do not know as she
has ever been accused of such a thing, but there
is something uncanny and disagreeable about her,

which I at once understood when I one day caught her in the very act of going through a nest of eggs.

A pair of the least flycatchers, the bird which says *chebec, chebec*, and is a small edition of the pewee, one season built their nest where I had them for many hours each day under my observation. The nest was a very snug and compact structure placed in the forks of a small maple about twelve feet from the ground. The season before, a red squirrel had harried the nest of a wood thrush in this same tree, and I was apprehensive that he would serve the flycatchers the same trick; so, as I sat with my book in a summer-house near by, I kept my loaded gun within easy reach. One egg was laid, and the next morning, as I made my daily inspection of the nest, only a fragment of its empty shell was to be found. This I removed, mentally imprecating the rogue of a red squirrel. The birds were much disturbed by the event, but did not desert the nest, as I had feared they would, but after much inspection of it, and many consultations together, concluded, it seems, to try again. Two more eggs were laid, when one day I heard the birds utter a sharp cry, and on looking up I saw a catbird perched upon the rim of the nest, hastily devouring the eggs. I soon regretted my precipitation in killing her, because such interference is generally unwise. It turned out that she had a nest of her own with five eggs, in a spruce-tree near my window.

Then this pair of little flycatchers did what I

had never seen birds do before: they pulled the
nest to pieces and rebuilt it in a peach-tree not
many rods away, where a brood was successfully
reared. The nest was here exposed to the direct
rays of the noonday sun, and, to shield her young
when the heat was greatest, the mother bird would
stand above them with wings slightly spread, as
other birds have been known to do under like circumstances.

To what extent the catbird is a nest-robber I
have no evidence; but that feline mew of hers, and
that flirting, flexible tail, suggest something not
entirely bird-like.

Probably the darkest tragedy of the nest is
enacted when a snake plunders it. All birds and
animals, so far as I have observed, behave in a
peculiar manner toward a snake. They seem to
feel something of the same loathing toward it that
the human species experience. The bark of a dog
when he encounters a snake is different from that
which he gives out on any other occasion; it is a
mingled note of alarm, inquiry, and disgust.

One day a tragedy was enacted a few yards from
where I was sitting with a book: two song sparrows
were trying to defend their nest against a black
snake. The curious, interrogating note of a chicken
who had suddenly come upon the scene in his walk
first caused me to look up from my reading. There
were the sparrows, with wings raised in a way
peculiarly expressive of horror and dismay, rushing
about a low clump of grass and bushes. Then,

looking more closely, I saw the glistening form of
the black snake, and the quick movement of his
head as he tried to seize the birds. The sparrows
darted about and through the grass and weeds, trying to beat the snake off. Their tails and wings
were spread, and, panting with the heat and the
desperate struggle, they presented a most singular
spectacle. They uttered no cry, not a sound escaped them; they were plainly speechless with horror and dismay. Not once did they drop their
wings, and the peculiar expression of those uplifted
palms, as it were, I shall never forget. It occurred
to me that perhaps here was a case of attempted
bird-charming on the part of the snake, so I looked
on from behind the fence. The birds charged the
snake and harassed him from every side, but were
evidently under no spell save that of courage in
defending their nest. Every moment or two I
could see the head and neck of the serpent make
a sweep at the birds, when the one struck at would
fall back, and the other would renew the assault
from the rear. There appeared to be little danger
that the snake could strike and hold one of the
birds, though I trembled for them, they were so
bold and approached so near to the snake's head.
Time and again he sprang at them, but without
success. How the poor things panted, and held
up their wings appealingly! Then the snake glided
off to the near fence, barely escaping the stone
which I hurled at him. I found the nest rifled
and deranged; whether it had contained eggs or

young, I know not. The male sparrow had cheered
me many a day with his song, and I blamed myself
for not having rushed at once to the rescue, when
the arch enemy was upon him. There is probably
little truth in the popular notion that snakes charm
birds. The black snake is the most subtle, alert,
and devilish of our snakes, and I have never seen
him have any but young, helpless birds in his
mouth.

We have one parasitical bird, the cowbird, so
called because it walks about amid the grazing cattle
and seizes the insects which their heavy tread sets
going, which is an enemy of most of the smaller
birds. It drops its egg in the nest of the song
sparrow, the social sparrow, the snowbird, the
vireos, and the wood-warblers, and as a rule it is
the only egg in the nest that issues successfully.
Either the eggs of the rightful owner of the nest
are not hatched, or else the young are overridden
and overreached by the parasite, and perish prematurely.

Among the worst enemies of our birds are the
so-called "collectors," men who plunder nests and
murder their owners in the name of science. Not
the genuine ornithologist, for no one is more careful
of squandering bird life than he; but the sham
ornithologist, the man whose vanity or affectation
happens to take an ornithological turn. He is
seized with an itching for a collection of eggs and
birds because it happens to be the fashion, or because it gives him the air of a man of science. But

in the majority of cases the motive is a mercenary
one; the collector expects to sell these spoils of the
groves and orchards. Robbing nests and killing
birds becomes a business with him. He goes about
it systematically, and becomes an expert in circumventing and slaying our songsters. Every town of
any considerable size is infested with one or more
of these bird highwaymen, and every nest in the
country round about that the wretches can lay hands
on is harried. Their professional term for a nest
of eggs is "a clutch," a word that well expresses
the work of their grasping, murderous fingers.
They clutch and destroy in the germ the life and
music of the woodlands. Certain of our natural
history journals are mainly organs of communica-
tion between these human weasels. They record
their exploits at nest-robbing and bird-slaying in
their columns. One collector tells with gusto how
he "worked his way" through an orchard, ransack-
ing every tree and leaving, as he believed, not one
nest behind him. He had better not be caught
working his way through my orchard. Another
gloats over the number of Connecticut warblers —
a rare bird — he killed in one season in Massachu-
setts. Another tells how a mockingbird appeared
in southern New England and was hunted down by
himself and friend, its eggs "clutched," and the
bird killed. Who knows how much the bird-lovers
of New England lost by that foul deed! The progeny of the birds would probably have returned to
Connecticut to breed, and their progeny, or a part

of them, the same, till in time the famous Southern
songster would have become a regular visitant to
New England.   In the same journal still another
collector describes minutely how he outwitted three
hummingbirds and captured their nests and eggs,
— a clutch he was very proud of.   A Massachu-
setts bird-harrier boasts of his clutch of the eggs of
that dainty little warbler, the blue yellow-back.
One season he took two sets, the next five sets, the
next four sets, beside some single eggs, and the
next season four sets, and says he might have found
more had he had more time.   One season he took,
in about twenty days, three sets from one tree.   I
have heard of a collector who boasted of having
taken one hundred sets of the eggs of the marsh
wren in a single day; of another who took, in the
same time, thirty nests of the yellow-breasted chat;
and of still another who claimed to have taken one
thousand sets of eggs of different birds in one season.   A large business has grown up under the
influence of this collecting craze.   One dealer in
eggs has those of over five hundred species.   He
says that his business in 1883 was twice that of
1882; in 1884 it was twice that of 1883, and so
on.   Collectors vie with each other in the extent
and variety of their cabinets.   They not only obtain
eggs in sets, but aim to have a number of sets of
the same bird, so as to show all possible variations.
I hear of a private collection that contains twelve
sets of kingbirds' eggs, eight sets of house wrens'
eggs, four sets of mockingbirds' eggs, etc.; sets of

eggs taken in low trees, high trees, medium trees; spotted sets, dark sets, plain sets, and light sets of the same species of bird. Many collections are made on this latter plan.

Thus are our birds hunted and cut off, and all in the name of science; as if science had not long ago finished with these birds. She has weighed and measured and dissected and described them, and their nests and eggs, and placed them in her cabinet; and the interest of science and of humanity now demands that this wholesale nest-robbing cease: These incidents I have given above, it is true, are but drops in the bucket, but the bucket would be more than full if we could get all the facts. Where one man publishes his notes, hundreds, perhaps thousands, say nothing, but go as silently about their nest-robbing as weasels.

It is true that the student of ornithology often feels compelled to take bird life. It is not an easy matter to "name all the birds without a gun," though an opera-glass will often render identification entirely certain, and leave the songster unharmed; but, once having mastered the birds, the true ornithologist leaves his gun at home. This view of the case may not be agreeable to that desiccated mortal called the "closet naturalist," but for my own part the closet naturalist is a person with whom I have very little sympathy. He is about the most wearisome and profitless creature in existence. With his piles of skins, his cases of eggs, his laborious feather-splitting, and his outlandish nomenclature, he is not only the enemy of the birds, but the enemy of all those who would know them rightly.

Not the collectors alone are to blame for the diminishing numbers of our wild birds, but a large share of the responsibility rests upon quite a different class of persons, namely, the milliners. False taste in dress is as destructive to our feathered friends as are false aims in science. It is said that the traffic in the skins of our brighter-plumaged birds, arising from their use by the milliners, reaches to hundreds of thousands annually. I am told of one middleman who collected from the shooters in one district, in four months, seventy thousand skins. It is a barbarous taste that craves this kind of ornamentation. Think of a woman or girl of real refinement appearing upon the street with her head-gear adorned with the scalps of our songsters!

It is probably true that the number of our birds destroyed by man is but a small percentage of the number cut off by their natural enemies; but it is to be remembered that those he destroys are in addition to those thus cut off, and that it is this extra or artificial destruction that disturbs the balance of nature. The operation of natural causes keeps the birds in check, but the greed of the collectors and milliners tends to their extinction.

I can pardon a man who wishes to make a collection of eggs and birds for his own private use, if he will content himself with one or two specimens of a kind, though he will find any collection much less satisfactory and less valuable than he imagines; but the professional nest-robber and skin-collector should be put down, either by legislation or with dogs and shotguns.

I have remarked above that there is probably very little truth in the popular notion that snakes can "charm" birds. But two of my correspondents have each furnished me with an incident from his own experience which seems to confirm the popular belief. One of them writes from Georgia as follows: —

"Some twenty-eight years ago I was in Calaveras County, California, engaged in cutting lumber. One day, in coming out of the camp or cabin, my attention was attracted to the curious action of a quail in the air, which, instead of flying low and straight ahead as usual, was some fifty feet high, flying in a circle, and uttering cries of distress. I watched the bird and saw it gradually descend, and following with my eye in a line from the bird to the ground, saw a large snake with head erect and some ten or twelve inches above the ground, and mouth wide open, and, as far as I could see, gazing intently on the quail (I was about thirty feet from the snake). The quail gradually descended, its circles growing smaller and smaller, and all the time uttering cries of distress, until its feet were within two or three inches of the mouth of the snake, when I threw a stone, and, though not hitting the snake, yet struck the ground so near as to frighten him, and he gradually started off. The quail, however, fell to the ground, apparently lifeless. I went forward and picked it up, and found it was thoroughly overcome with fright, its little heart beating as if it would burst through the skin. After holding it in my hand a few moments it flew away. I then tried to find the snake, but could not. I am unable to say whether the snake was venomous, or belonged to the constricting family, like the black snake. I can well recollect it was large and moved off rather slow. As I had never seen anything of the kind before, it made a great impression on my mind, and, after the lapse of so long a time, the incident appears as vivid to me as though it had occurred yesterday."

It is not probable that the snake had its mouth open; its darting tongue may have given that impression.

The other incident comes to me from Vermont. "While returning from church in 1876," says the writer, "as I was crossing a bridge . . . I noticed a striped snake in the act of charming a song sparrow. They were both upon the sand beneath the bridge. The snake kept his head swaying slowly from side to side and darted his tongue out continually. The bird, not over a foot away, was facing the snake, hopping from one foot to the other, and uttering a dissatisfied little chirp. I watched them till the snake seized the bird, having gradually drawn nearer. As he seized it, I leaped over the side of the bridge; the snake glided away, and I took up the bird, which he had dropped. It was too frightened to try to fly, and I carried it nearly a mile before it flew from my open hand."

If these observers are quite sure of what they saw, then undoubtedly snakes have the power to draw birds within their grasp. I remember that my mother once told me that while gathering wild strawberries she had on one occasion come upon a bird fluttering about the head of a snake as if held there by a spell. On her appearance, the snake lowered its head and made off, and the panting bird flew away. A black snake was killed by a neighbor of mine which had swallowed a full-grown red squirrel, probably captured by the same power of fascination.

XII

PHASES OF FARM LIFE

I HAVE thought that a good test of civilization, perhaps one of the best, is country life. Where country life is safe and enjoyable, where many of the conveniences and appliances of the town are joined to the large freedom and large benefits of the country, a high state of civilization prevails. Is there any proper country life in Spain, in Mexico, in the South American States? Man has always dwelt in cities, but he has not always in the same sense been a dweller in the country. Rude and barbarous people build cities. Hence, paradoxical as it may seem, the city is older than the country. Truly, man made the city, and after he became sufficiently civilized, not afraid of solitude, and knew on what terms to live with nature, God promoted him to life in the country. The necessities of defense, the fear of enemies, built the first city, built Rome, Athens, Carthage, Paris. The weaker the law, the stronger the city. After Cain slew Abel he went out and built a city, and murder or the fear of murder, robbery or the fear of robbery, have built most of the cities since. Penetrate into the heart of Africa, and you will find the people, or tribes, all living in villages or little cities. You step from the jungle or forest into the town; there is no country. The best and most hopeful feature in any people is undoubtedly the instinct that leads them to the country and to take root there, and not that which sends them flocking to the town and its distractions.

The lighter the snow, the more it drifts; and the more frivolous the people, the more they are blown by one wind or another into towns and cities.

The only notable exception I recall to city life preceding country life is furnished by the ancient Germans, of whom Tacitus says that they had no cities or contiguous settlements. "They dwell scattered and separate, as a spring, a meadow, or a grove may chance to invite them. Their villages are laid out, not like ours [the Romans] in rows of adjoining buildings, but every one surrounds his house with a vacant space, either by way of security, or against fire, or through ignorance of the art of building."

These ancient Germans were indeed true countrymen. Little wonder that they overran the empire of the city-loving Romans, and finally sacked Rome itself. How hairy and hardy and virile they were! In the same way is the more fresh and vigorous blood of the country always making eruptions into the city. The Goths and Vandals from the woods and the farms, — what would Rome do without them, after all? The city rapidly uses men up; families run out, man becomes sophisticated and

feeble.   A fresh stream of humanity is always setting from the country into the city; a stream not
so fresh flows back again into the country, a stream
for the most part of jaded and pale humanity.   It
is arterial blood when it flows in, and venous blood
when it comes back.

A nation always begins to rot first in its great
cities, is indeed perhaps always rotting there, and
is saved only by the antiseptic virtues of fresh supplies of country blood.

But it is not of country life in general that I am
to speak, but of some phases of farm life, and of
farm life in my native State.

Many of the early settlers of New York were
from New England, Connecticut perhaps sending
out the most.   My own ancestors were from the
latter State.   The Connecticut emigrant usually
made his first stop in our river counties, Putnam,
Dutchess, or Columbia.   If he failed to find his
place there, he made another flight to Orange, to
Delaware, or to Schoharie County, where he generally stuck.   But the State early had one element
introduced into its rural and farm life not found
farther East, namely, the Holland Dutch.   These
gave features more or less picturesque to the country that are not observable in New England.   The
Dutch took root at various points along the Hudson,
and about Albany and in the Mohawk valley, and
remnants of their rural and domestic architecture
may still be seen in these sections of the State.   A

Dutch barn became proverbial. "As broad as a Dutch barn" was a phrase that, when applied to the person of a man or woman, left room for little more to be said. The main feature of these barns was their enormous expansion of roof. It was a comfort to look at them, they suggested such shelter and protection. The eaves were very low and the ridge-pole very high. Long rafters and short posts gave them a quaint, short-waisted, grandmotherly look. They were nearly square, and stood very broad upon the ground. Their form was doubtless suggested by the damper climate of the Old World, where the grain and hay, instead of being packed in deep solid mows, used to be spread upon poles and exposed to the currents of air under the roof. Surface and not cubic capacity is more important in these matters in Holland than in this country. Our farmers have found that, in a climate where there is so much weather as with us, the less roof you have the better. Roofs will leak, and cured hay will keep sweet in a mow of any depth and size in our dry atmosphere.

The Dutch barn was the most picturesque barn that has been built, especially when thatched with straw, as they nearly all were, and forming one side of an inclosure of lower roofs or sheds also covered with straw, beneath which the cattle took refuge from the winter storms. Its immense, unpainted gable, cut with holes for the swallows, was like a section of a respectable-sized hill, and its roof like its slope. Its great doors always had a hood pro-

jecting over them, and the doors themselves were
divided horizontally into upper and lower halves;
the upper halves very frequently being left open,
through which you caught a glimpse of the mows
of hay, or the twinkle of flails when the grain was
being threshed.

The old Dutch farmhouses, too, were always
pleasing to look upon.   They were low, often made
of stone, with deep window-jambs and great family
fireplaces.   The outside door, like that of the barn,
was always divided into upper and lower halves.
When the weather permitted, the upper half could
stand open, giving light and air without the cold
draught over the floor where the children were play-
ing that our wide-swung doors admit.   This feature of the Dutch house and barn certainly merits
preservation in our modern buildings.

The large, unpainted timber barns that succeeded
the first Yankee settlers' log stables were also picturesque, especially when a lean-to for the cow-
stable was added, and the roof carried down with a
long sweep over it; or when the barn was flanked
by an open shed with a hayloft above it, where
the hens cackled and hid their nests, and from the
open window of which the hay was always hanging.

Then the great timbers of these barns and the
Dutch barn, hewn from maple or birch or oak trees
from the primitive woods, and put in place by the
combined strength of all the brawny arms in the
neighborhood when the barn was raised, — timbers
strong enough and heavy enough for docks and

quays, and that have absorbed the odors of the hay
and grain until they look ripe and mellow and full
of the pleasing sentiment of the great, sturdy,
bountiful interior! The "big beam" has become
smooth and polished from the hay that has been
pitched over it, and the sweaty, sturdy forms that
have crossed it. One feels that he would like a
piece of furniture — a chair, or a table, or a writing-
desk, a bedstead, or a wainscoting — made from
these long-seasoned, long-tried, richly-toned timbers
of the old barn. But the smart-painted, natty barn
that follows the humbler structure, with its glazed
windows, its ornamented ventilator and gilded weather vane, — who cares to contemplate it? The
wise human eye loves modesty and humility; loves
plain, simple structures; loves the unpainted barn
that took no thought of itself, or the dwelling that
looks inward and not outward; is offended when the
farm-buildings get above their business and aspire
to be something on their own account, suggesting,
not cattle and crops and plain living, but the vani-
ties of the town and the pride of dress and equipage.

Indeed, the picturesque in human affairs and
occupations is always born of love and humility, as
it is in art or literature; and it quickly takes to
itself wings and flies away at the advent of pride,
or any selfish or unworthy motive. The more directly the farm savors of the farmer, the more the
fields and buildings are redolent of human care and
toil, without any thought of the passer-by, the more
we delight in the contemplation of it.

It is unquestionably true that farm life and farm scenes in this country are less picturesque than they were fifty or one hundred years ago. This is owing partly to the advent of machinery, which enables the farmer to do so much of his work by proxy, and hence removes him farther from the soil, and partly to the growing distaste for the occupation among our people. The old settlers — our fathers and grandfathers — loved the farm, and had no thoughts above it; but the later generations are looking to the town and its fashions, and only waiting for a chance to flee thither. Then pioneer life is always more or less picturesque; there is no room for vain and foolish thoughts; it is a hard battle, and the people have no time to think about appearances. When my grandfather and grandmother came into the country where they reared their family and passed their days, they cut a road through the woods and brought all their worldly gear on a sled drawn by a yoke of oxen. Their neighbors helped them build a house of logs, with a roof of black-ash bark and a floor of hewn white-ash plank. A great stone chimney and fireplace — the mortar of red clay — gave light and warmth, and cooked the meat and baked the bread, when there was any to cook or to bake. Here they lived and reared their family, and found life sweet. Their unworthy descendant, yielding to the inherited love of the soil, flees the city and its artificial ways, and gets a few acres in the country, where he proposes to engage in the pursuit supposed to be free to every American citizen, — the pursuit of happiness. The humble old farmhouse is discarded, and a smart, modern country-house put up. Walks and roads are made and graveled; trees and hedges are planted; the rustic old barn is rehabilitated; and, after it is all fixed, the uneasy proprietor stands off and looks, and calculates by how much he has missed the picturesque, at which he aimed. Our new houses undoubtedly have greater comforts and conveniences than the old; and, if we could keep our pride and vanity in abeyance and forget that all the world is looking on, they might have beauty also.

The man that forgets himself, he is the man we like; and the dwelling that forgets itself, in its purpose to shelter and protect its inmates and make them feel at home in it, is the dwelling that fills the eye. When you see one of the great cathedrals, you know that it was not pride that animated these builders, but fear and worship; but when you see the house of the rich farmer, or of the millionaire from the city, you see the pride of money and the insolence of social power.

Machinery, I say, has taken away some of the picturesque features of farm life. How much soever we may admire machinery and the faculty of mechanical invention, there is no machine like a man; and the work done directly by his hands, the things made or fashioned by them, have a virtue and a quality that cannot be imparted by machinery. The line of mowers in the meadows, with the straight swaths behind them, are more picturesque than the "Clipper" or "Buckeye" mower, with its team and driver. So are the flails of the threshers, chasing each other through the air, more pleasing to the eye and the ear than the machine, with its uproar, its choking clouds of dust, and its general hurly-burly.

Sometimes the threshing was done in the open air, upon a broad rock, or a smooth, dry plat of greensward; and it is occasionally done there yet, especially the threshing of the buckwheat crop, by a farmer who has not a good barn floor, or who cannot afford to hire the machine. The flail makes a louder *thud* in the fields than you would imagine; and in the splendid October weather it is a pleasing spectacle to behold the gathering of the ruddy crop, and three or four lithe figures beating out the grain with their flails in some sheltered nook, or some grassy lane lined with cedars. When there are three flails beating together it makes lively music; and when there are four they follow each other so fast that it is a continuous roll of sound, and it requires a very steady stroke not to hit or get hit by the others. There is just room and time to get your blow in, and that is all. When one flail is upon the straw, another has just left it, another is half way down, and the fourth is high and straight in the air. It is like a swiftly revolving wheel that delivers four blows at each revolution. Threshing, like mowing, goes much easier in company than when alone; yet many a farmer or laborer

spends nearly all the late fall and winter days shut
in the barn, pounding doggedly upon the endless
sheaves of oats and rye.

When the farmers made "bees," as they did a
generation or two ago much more than they do
now, a picturesque element was added. There was
the stone bee, the husking bee, the "raising," the
"moving," etc. When the carpenters had got the
timbers of the house or barn ready, and the foundation was prepared, then the neighbors for miles
about were invited to come to the "raisin'." The
afternoon was the time chosen. The forenoon was
occupied by the carpenter and farm hands in putting the sills and "sleepers" in place ("sleepers,"
what a good name for those rude hewn timbers that
lie under the floor in the darkness and silence!).
When the hands arrived, the great beams and posts
and joists and braces were carried to their place on
the platform, and the first "bent," as it was called,
was put together and pinned by oak pins that the
boys brought. Then pike poles are distributed,
the men, fifteen or twenty of them, arranged in a
line abreast of the bent; the boss carpenter steadies
and guides the corner post and gives the word of
command, — "Take holt, boys!" "Now, set her
up!" "Up with her!" "Up she goes!" When
it gets shoulder high it becomes heavy, and there
is a pause. The pikes are brought into requisition;
every man gets a good hold and braces himself, and
waits for the words. "All together now;" shouts
the captain, "Heave her up!" "He-o-he!" (heave-

all, — heave), "he-o-he," at the top of his voice,
every man doing his best.   Slowly the great timbers go up; louder grows the word of command,
till the bent is up.   Then it is plumbed and stay-
lathed, and another is put together and raised in
the same way, till they are all up.   Then comes
the putting on the great plates, — timbers that run
lengthwise of the building and match the sills
below.   Then, if there is time, the putting up of
the rafters.   In every neighborhood there was always some man who was especially useful at "raisin's."   He was bold and strong and quick.   He
helped guide and superintend the work.   He was
the first one up on the bent, catching a pin or a
brace and putting it in place.   He walked the lofty
and perilous plate, with the great beetle in hand;
put the pins in the holes, and, swinging the heavy
instrument through the air, drove the pins home.
He was as much at home up there as a squirrel.

Now that balloon frames are mainly used for
houses, and lighter sawed timbers for barns, the
old-fashioned raising is rarely witnessed.

Then the moving was an event, too.   A farmer
had a barn to move, or wanted to build a new
house on the site of the old one, and the latter must
be drawn to one side.   Now this work is done with
pulleys and rollers by a few men and a horse; then
the building was drawn by sheer bovine strength.
Every man that had a yoke of cattle in the country
round about was invited to assist.   The barn or
house was pried up and great runners, cut in the

woods, placed under it, and under the runners were placed skids. To these runners it was securely chained and pinned; then the cattle — stags, steers, and oxen, in two long lines, one at each runner — were hitched fast, and, while men and boys aided with great levers, the word to go was given. Slowly the two lines of bulky cattle straightened and settled into their bows; the big chains that wrapped the runners tightened, a dozen or more "gads" were flourished, a dozen or more lusty throats urged their teams at the top of their voices, when there was a creak or a groan as the building stirred. Then the drivers redoubled their efforts; there was a perfect Babel of discordant sounds; the oxen bent to the work, their eyes bulged, their nostrils distended; the lookers-on cheered, and away went the old house or barn as nimbly as a boy on a hand-sled. Not always, however; sometimes the chains would break, or one runner strike a rock, or bury itself in the earth. There were generally enough mishaps or delays to make it interesting.

In the section of the State of which I write, flax used to be grown, and cloth for shirts and trowsers, and towels and sheets, etc., woven from it. It was no laughing matter for the farm-boy to break in his shirt or trowsers those days. The hair shirts in which the old monks used to mortify the flesh could not have been much before them in this mortifying particular. But after the bits of shives and sticks were subdued, and the knots humbled by use and the washboard, they were good garments. If you lost your hold in a tree and your shirt caught on a knot or limb, it would save you.

But when has any one seen a crackle, or a swingling-knife, or a hetchel, or a distaff, and where can one get some tow for strings or for gun-wadding, or some swingling-tow for a bonfire? The quill-wheel, and the spinning-wheel, and the loom are heard no more among us. The last I knew of a certain hetchel, it was nailed up behind the old sheep that did the churning; and when he was disposed to shirk or hang back and stop the machine, it was always ready to spur him up in no uncertain manner. The old loom became a hen-roost in an outbuilding; and the crackle upon which the flax was broken, — where, oh, where is it?

When the produce of the farm was taken a long distance to market, — that was an event, too; the carrying away of the butter in the fall, for instance, to the river, a journey that occupied both ways four days. Then the family marketing was done in a few groceries. Some cloth, new caps and boots for the boys, and a dress, or a shawl, or a cloak for the girls were brought back, besides news and adventure, and strange tidings of the distant world. The farmer was days in getting ready to start; food was prepared and put in a box to stand him on the journey, so as to lessen the hotel expenses, and oats put up for the horses. The butter was loaded up overnight, and in the cold November morning, long before it was light, he was up and off. I seem to hear the wagon yet, its slow rattle over the frozen

ground diminishing in the distance. On the fourth
day toward night all grew expectant of his return,
but it was usually dark before his wagon was heard
coming down the hill, or his voice from before the
door summoning a light. When the boys got big
enough, one after the other accompanied him each
year, until all had made the famous journey and
seen the great river and the steamboats, and the
thousand and one marvels of the far-away town.
When it came my turn to go, I was in a great state
of excitement for a week beforehand, for fear my
clothes would not be ready, or else that it would
be too cold, or else that the world would come to
an end before the time fixed for starting. The day
previous I roamed the woods in quest of game to
supply my bill of fare on the way, and was lucky
enough to shoot a partridge and an owl, though the
latter I did not take. Perched high on a "spring-
board." I made the journey, and saw more sights
and wonders than I have ever seen on a journey
since, or ever expect to again.

But now all this is changed. The railroad has
found its way through or near every settlement, and
marvels and wonders are cheap. Still, the essential
charm of the farm remains and always will remain:
the care of crops, and of cattle, and of orchards,
bees, and fowls; the clearing and improving of the
ground; the building of barns and houses; the direct contact with the soil and with the elements;
the watching of the clouds and of the weather; the
privacies with nature, with bird, beast, and plant;

and the close acquaintance with the heart and virtue of the world. The farmer should be the true
naturalist; the book in which it is all written is
open before him night and day, and how sweet and
wholesome all his knowledge is!

The predominant feature of farm life in New
York, as in other States, is always given by some
local industry of one kind or another. In many
of the high cold counties in the eastern centre of
the State, this ruling industry is hop - growing;
in the western, it is grain and fruit growing; in
sections along the Hudson, it is small-fruit growing, as berries, currants, grapes; in other counties,
it is milk and butter; in others, quarrying flag-
ging-stone. I recently visited a section of Ulster
County, where everybody seemed getting out hoop-
poles and making hoops. The only talk was of
hoops, hoops! Every team that went by had a
load or was going for a load of hoops. The principal fuel was hoop-shavings or discarded hoop-poles.
No man had any money until he sold his hoops.
When a farmer went to town to get some grain, or
a pair of boots, or a dress for his wife, he took
a load of hoops. People stole hoops and poached
for hoops, and bought, and sold, and speculated in
hoops. If there was a corner it was in hoops;
big hoops, little hoops, hoops for kegs, and firkins,
and barrels, and hogsheads, and pipes; hickory
hoops, birch hoops, ash hoops, chestnut hoops, hoops
enough to go around the world. Another place it
was shingle, shingle; everybody was shaving hemlock shingle.

In most of the eastern counties of the State, the
interest and profit of the farm revolve about the
cow. The dairy is the one great matter, — for
milk, when milk can be shipped to the New York
market, and for butter when it cannot. Great barns
and stables and milking-sheds, and immense meadows and cattle on a thousand hills, are the prominent agricultural features of these sections of the
country. Good grass and good water are the two
indispensables to successful dairying. And the two
generally go together. Where there are plenty of
copious cold springs, there is no dearth of grass.
When the cattle are compelled to browse upon
weeds and various wild growths, the milk and butter will betray it in the flavor. Tender, juicy
grass, the ruddy blossoming clover, or the fragrant,
well-cured hay, make the delicious milk and the
sweet butter. Then there is a charm about a natural pastoral country that belongs to no other. Go
through Orange County in May and see the vivid
emerald of the smooth fields and hills. It is a new
experience of the beauty and effectiveness of simple
grass. And this grass has rare virtues, too, and
imparts a flavor to the milk and butter that has
made them famous.

Along all the sources of the Delaware the land
flows with milk, if not with honey. The grass is
excellent, except in times of protracted drought,
and then the browsings in the beech and birch
woods are good substitute. Butter is the staple
product. Every housewife is or wants to be a

famous butter-maker, and Delaware County butter
rivals Orange in market.   It is a high, cool grazing country.   The farms lie tilted up against the
sides of the mountain or lapping over the hills,
striped or checked with stone wall, and presenting
to the eye long stretches of pasture and meadow
land, alternating with plowed fields and patches of
waving grain.   Few of their features are picturesque; they are bare, broad, and simple.   The
farmhouse gets itself a coat of white paint, and
green blinds to the windows, and the barn and
wagon-house a coat of red paint with white trim-
mings, as soon as possible.   A penstock flows by
the doorway, rows of tin pans sun themselves in
the yard, and the great wheel of the churning
machine flanks the milk-house, or rattles behind it.
The winters are severe, the snow deep.   The principal fuel is still wood, — beech, birch, and maple.
It is hauled off the mountain in great logs when
the first November or December snows come, and
cut up and piled in the wood-houses and under a
shed.   Here the axe still rules the winter, and it
may be heard all day and every day upon the wood-
pile, or echoing through the frost-bound wood, the
coat of the chopper hanging to a limb, and his
white chips strewing the snow.

Many cattle need much hay; hence in dairy sections haying is the period of "storm and stress" in
the farmer's year.   To get the hay in, in good condition, and before the grass gets too ripe, is a great
matter.   All the energies and resources of the farm

are bent to this purpose. It is a thirty or forty
day war, in which the farmer and his "hands" are
pitted against the heat and the rain and the legions
of timothy and clover. Everything about it has
the urge, the hurry, the excitement of a battle.
Outside help is procured; men flock in from adjoining counties, where the ruling industry is something
else and is less imperative; coopers, blacksmiths,
and laborers of various kinds drop their tools, and
take down their scythes and go in quest of a job in
haying. Every man is expected to pitch his en-
deavors in a little higher key than at any other
kind of work. The wages are extra, and the work
must correspond. The men are in the meadow by
half-past four or five in the morning, and mow an
hour or two before breakfast. A good mower is
proud of his skill. He does not "lop in," and his
"pointing out" is perfect, and you can hardly see
the ribs of his swath. He stands up to his grass
and strikes level and sure. He will turn a double
down through the stoutest grass, and when the hay
is raked away you will not find a spear left standing. The Americans are — or were — the best
mowers. A foreigner could never quite give the
masterly touch. The hayfield has its code. One
man must not take another's swath unless he expects to be crowded. Each expects to take his turn
leading the band. The scythe may be so whet as
to ring out a saucy challenge to the rest. It is not
good manners to mow up too close to your neighbor, unless you are trying to keep out of the way

of the man behind you. Many a race has been brought on by some one being a little indiscreet in this respect. Two men may mow all day together under the impression that each is trying to put the other through. The one that leads strikes out briskly, and the other, not to be outdone, follows close. Thus the blood of each is soon up; a little heat begets more heat, and it is fairly a race before long. It is a great ignominy to be mowed out of your swath. Hay-gathering is clean, manly work all through. Young fellows work in haying who do not do another stroke on the farm the whole year. It is a gymnasium in the meadows and under the summer sky. How full of pictures, too! — the smooth slopes dotted with cocks with lengthening shadows; the great, broad-backed, soft-cheeked loads, moving along the lanes and brushing under the trees; the unfinished stack with forkfuls of hay being handed up its sides to the builder, and when finished the shape of a great pear, with a pole in the top for the stem. Maybe in the fall and winter the calves and yearlings will hover around it and gnaw its base until it overhangs them and shelters them from the storm. Or the farmer will "fodder" his cows there, — one of the most picturesque scenes to be witnessed on the farm, — twenty or thirty or forty milchers filing along toward the stack in the field, or clustered about it, waiting the promised bite. In great, green flakes the hay is rolled off, and distributed about in small heaps upon the unspotted snow. After the cattle

have eaten, the birds — snow buntings and redpolls — come and pick up the crumbs, the seeds of
the grasses and weeds. At night the fox and the
owl come for mice.

What a beautiful path the cows make through
the snow to the stack or to the spring under the
hill! — always more or less wayward, but broad
and firm, and carved and indented by a multitude
of rounded hoofs.

In fact, the cow is the true pathfinder and path-
maker. She has the leisurely, deliberate movement
that insures an easy and a safe way. Follow her
trail through the woods, and you have the best, if
not the shortest, course. How she beats down the
brush and briers and wears away even the roots of
the trees! A herd of cows left to themselves fall
naturally into single file, and a hundred or more
hoofs are not long in smoothing and compacting
almost any surface.

Indeed, all the ways and doings of cattle are
pleasant to look upon, whether grazing in the pasture, or browsing in the woods, or ruminating under
the trees, or feeding in the stall, or reposing upon
the knolls. There is virtue in the cow; she is full
of goodness; a wholesome odor exhales from her;
the whole landscape looks out of her soft eyes; the
quality and the aroma of miles of meadow and pasture lands are in her presence and products. I had
rather have the care of cattle than be the keeper
of the great seal of the nation. Where the cow is,
there is Arcadia; so far as her influence prevails,

there is contentment, humility, and sweet, homely
life.

Blessed is he whose youth was passed upon the
farm, and if it was a dairy farm his memories will
be all the more fragrant. The driving of the cows
to and from the pasture, every day and every season
for years, — how much of summer and of nature
he got into him on these journeys! What rambles
and excursions did this errand furnish the excuse
for! The birds and birds' nests, the berries, the
squirrels, the woodchucks, the beech woods with
their treasures into which the cows loved so to
wander and to browse, the fragrant wintergreens
and a hundred nameless adventures, all strung upon
that brief journey of half a mile to and from the
remote pastures. Sometimes one cow or two will
be missing when the herd is brought home at
night; then to hunt them up is another adventure.
My grandfather went out one night to look up an
absentee from the yard, when he heard something
in the brush, and out stepped a bear into the path
before him.

Every Sunday morning the cows were salted.
The farm-boy would take a pail with three or four
quarts of coarse salt, and, followed by the eager
herd, go to the field and deposit the salt in hand-
fuls upon smooth stones and rocks and upon clean
places on the turf. If you want to know how good
salt is, see a cow eat it. She gives the true saline
smack. How she dwells upon it, and gnaws the
sward and licks the stones where it has been depos-

ited! The cow is the most delightful feeder among animals. It makes one's mouth water to see her eat pumpkins, and to see her at a pile of apples is distracting. How she sweeps off the delectable grass! The sound of her grazing is appetizing; the grass betrays all its sweetness and succulency in parting under her sickle.

The region of which I write abounds in sheep also. Sheep love high, cool, breezy lands. Their range is generally much above that of cattle. Their sharp noses will find picking where a cow would fare poorly indeed. Hence most farmers utilize their high, wild, and mountain lands by keeping a small flock of sheep. But they are the outlaws of the farm and are seldom within bounds. They make many lively expeditions for the farm-boy, — driving them out of mischief, hunting them up in the mountains, or salting them on the breezy hills. Then there is the annual sheep-washing, when on a warm day in May or early June the whole herd is driven a mile or more to a suitable pool in the creek, and one by one doused and washed and rinsed in the water. We used to wash below an old grist-mill, and it was a pleasing spectacle, — the mill, the dam, the overhanging rocks and trees, the round, deep pool, and the huddled and frightened sheep.

One of the features of farm life peculiar to this country, and one of the most picturesque of them all, is sugar-making in the maple woods in spring. This is the first work of the season, and to the

boys is more play than work. In the Old World,
and in more simple and imaginative times, how
such an occupation as this would have got into
literature, and how many legends and associations
would have clustered around it! It is woodsy, and
savors of the trees; it is an encampment among
the maples. Before the bud swells, before the
grass springs, before the plow is started, comes the
sugar harvest. It is the sequel of the bitter frost;
a sap-run is the sweet good-by of winter. It de-
notes a certain equipoise of the season; the heat of
the day fully balances the frost of the night. In
New York and New England the time of the sap
hovers about the vernal equinox, beginning a week
or ten days before, and continuing a week or ten
days after. As the days and nights get equal, the
heat and cold get equal, and the sap mounts. A
day that brings the bees out of the hive will bring
the sap out of the maple-tree. It is the fruit of
the equal marriage of the sun and frost. When the
frost is all out of the ground, and all the snow
gone from its surface, the flow stops. The thermometer must not rise above 38° or 40° by day,
or sink below 24° or 25° at night, with wind in
the northwest; a relaxing south wind, and the run
is over for the present. Sugar weather is crisp
weather. How the tin buckets glisten in the gray
woods; how the robins laugh; how the nuthatches
call; how lightly the thin blue smoke rises among
the trees! The squirrels are out of their dens; the
migrating water-fowls are streaming northward; the

sheep and cattle look wistfully toward the bare
fields; the tide of the season, in fact, is just beginning to rise.

Sap-letting does not seem to be an exhaustive
process to the trees, as the trees of a sugar-bush
appear to be as thrifty and as long-lived as other
trees. They come to have a maternal, large-waisted
look, from the wounds of the axe or the auger, and
that is about all.

In my sugar-making days, the sap was carried to
the boiling-place in pails by the aid of a neck-yoke
and stored in hogsheads, and boiled or evaporated
in immense kettles or caldrons set in huge stone
arches; now, the hogshead goes to the trees hauled
upon a sled by a team, and the sap is evaporated in
broad, shallow, sheet-iron pans, — a great saving of
fuel and of labor.

Many a farmer sits up all night boiling his sap,
when the run has been an extra good one, and a
lonely vigil he has of it amid the silent trees and
beside his wild hearth.   If he has a sap-house, as
is now so common, he may make himself fairly com-
fortable; and if a companion, he may have a good
time or a glorious wake.

Maple-sugar in its perfection is rarely seen, perhaps never seen, in the market.   When made in
large quantities and indifferently, it is dark and
coarse; but when made in small quantities — that
is, quickly from the first run of sap and properly
treated — it has a wild delicacy of flavor that no
other sweet can match.   What you smell in freshly

cut maple-wood, or taste in the blossom of the tree,
is in it. It is then, indeed, the distilled essence of
the tree. Made into syrup, it is white and clear
as clover-honey; and crystallized into sugar, it is
pure as the wax. The way to attain this result is
to evaporate the sap under cover in an enameled
kettle; when reduced about twelve times, allow it
to settle half a day or more; then clarify with milk
or the white of an egg. The product is virgin
syrup, or sugar worthy the table of the gods.

Perhaps the most heavy and laborious work of
the farm in the section of the State of which I
write is fence-building. But it is not unproductive
labor, as in the South or West, for the fence is of
stone, and the capacity of the soil for grass or grain
is, of course, increased by its construction. It is
killing two birds with one stone: a fence is had,
the best in the world, while the available area of
the field is enlarged. In fact, if there are ever
sermons in stones, it is when they are built into a
stone wall, — turning your hindrances into helps,
shielding your crops behind the obstacles to your
husbandry, making the enemies of the plow stand
guard over its products. This is the kind of farming worth imitating. A stone wall with a good
rock bottom will stand as long as a man lasts. Its
only enemy is the frost, and it works so gently
that it is not till after many years that its effect is
perceptible. An old farmer will walk with you
through his fields and say, "This wall I built at
such and such a time, or the first year I came on

the farm, or when I owned such and such a span of
horses," indicating a period thirty, forty, or fifty
years back. "This other, we built the summer so
and so worked for me," and he relates some incident, or mishap, or comical adventures that the
memory calls up. Every line of fence has a history; the mark of his plow or his crowbar is upon
the stones; the sweat of his early manhood put them
in place; in fact, the long black line covered with
lichens and in places tottering to the fall revives
long-gone scenes and events in the life of the farm.

The time for fence-building is usually between
seed-time and harvest, May and June; or in the
fall after the crops are gathered. The work has its
picturesque features, — the prying of rocks; supple
forms climbing or swinging from the end of the
great levers, or the blasting of the rocks with powder; the hauling of them into position with oxen
or horses, or with both; the picking of the stone
from the greensward; the bending, athletic form of
the wall-layers; the snug new fence creeping slowly
up the hill or across the field, absorbing the wind-
row of loose stones; and, when the work is done,
much ground reclaimed to the plow and the grass,
and a strong barrier erected.

It is a common complaint that the farm and
farm life are not appreciated by our people. We
long for the more elegant pursuits, or the ways and
fashions of the town. But the farmer has the most
sane and natural occupation, and ought to find life
sweeter, if less highly seasoned, than any other.

He alone, strictly speaking, has a home. How can
a man take root and thrive without land? He
writes his history upon his field. How many ties,
how many resources, he has, — his friendships with
his cattle, his team, his dog, his trees, the satisfaction in his growing crops, in his improved fields;
his intimacy with nature, with bird and beast, and
with the quickening elemental forces; his coöpera-
tions with the cloud, the sun, the seasons, heat,
wind, rain, frost! Nothing will take the various
social distempers which the city and artificial life
breed out of a man like farming, like direct and lov-
ing contact with the soil. It draws out the poison.
It humbles him, teaches him patience and reverence,
and restores the proper tone to his system.

Cling to the farm, make much of it, put yourself
into it, bestow your heart and your brain upon it,
so that it shall savor of you and radiate your virtue
after your day's work is done!

"Be thou diligent to know the state of thy flocks,
and look well to thy herds.

"For riches are not forever; and doth the crown
endure to every generation?

"The hay appeareth, and the tender grass show-
eth itself, and herbs of the mountains are gathered.

"The lambs are for thy clothing, and the goats
are the price of the field.

"And thou shalt have goat's milk enough for
thy food, for the food of thy household, and for
the maintenance for thy maidens."

XIII

ROOF—TREE

ONE of the greatest pleasures of life is to build a house for one's self. There is a peculiar satisfaction even in planting a tree from which you hope to eat the fruit, or in the shade of which you hope to repose. But how much greater the pleasure in planting the roof-tree, the tree that bears the golden apples of home and hospitality, and under the protection of which you hope to pass the remainder of your days! My grandmother said the happiest day of her life was when she found herself mistress of a little log-house in the woods. Grandfather and she had built it mainly with their own hands, and doubtless with as much eagerness and solicitude as the birds build their nests. It was made of birch and maple logs, the floor was of hewn logs, and its roof of black-ash bark. But it was home and fireside, a few square feet of the great, wild, inclement, inhospitable out-of-doors subdued and set about by four walls and made warm and redolent of human hearts. I notice how eager all men are in building their houses, how they linger about them, or even about their proposed sites. When the cellar is being dug, they want to take a hand in it; the earth evidently looks a little different, a little more friendly and congenial, than other earth. When the foundation walls are up and the first floor is rudely sketched by rough timbers, I see them walking pensively from one imaginary room to another, or sitting long and long, wrapped in sweet reverie, upon the naked joist. It is a favorite pastime to go there of a Sunday afternoon and linger fondly about; they take their friends or their neighbors and climb the skeleton stairs and look out of the vacant windows, and pass in and out of the just sketched doorways. How long the house is a-finishing! The heart moves in long before the workmen move out. Will the mason and the painter and the plumber never be through?

When a new house is going up in my vicinity, I find myself walking thitherward nearly every day to see how the work progresses. What pleasure to see the structure come into shape, and the architect's paper plans take form and substance in wood and stone! I like to see every piece fitted, every nail driven. I stand about till I am in the way of the carpenters or masons. Another new roof to shelter somebody from the storms, another four walls to keep the great cosmic out-of-doors at bay!

Though there is pleasure in building our house, or in seeing our neighbor build, yet the old houses look the best. Disguise it as one will, the new house is more or less a wound upon nature, and time must elapse for the wound to heal. Then, unless one builds with modesty and simplicity, and

with a due regard to the fitness of things, his house
will always be a wound, an object of offense upon
the fair face of the landscape. Indeed, to build a
house that shall not offend the wise eye, that shall
not put Nature and all her gentle divinities to
shame, is the great problem. In such matters, not
to displease the eye is to please the heart.

Probably the most that is to be aimed at in
domestic architecture is negative beauty, a condition
of things which invites or suggests beauty to those
who are capable of the sentiment, because a house,
truly viewed, is but a setting, a background, and is
not to be pushed to the front and made much of for
its own sake. It is for shelter, for comfort, for
health and hospitality, to eat in and sleep in, to be
born in and to die in, and it is to accord in appearance with homely every-day usages, and with natural, universal objects and scenes. Indeed, is anything but negative beauty to be aimed at in the
interior decorations as well? The hangings are but
a background for the pictures, and are to give tone
and atmosphere to the rooms; while the whole interior is but a background for the human form, and
for the domestic life to be lived there.

It may be observed that what we call beauty of
nature is mainly negative beauty; that is, the mass,
the huge rude background, made up of rocks, trees,
hills, mountains, plains, water, etc., has not beauty
as a positive quality, visible to all eyes, but affords
the mind the conditions of beauty, namely, health,
strength, fitness, etc., beauty being an *experience*

of the beholder. Some things, on the other hand,
as flowers, foliage, brilliant colors, sunsets, rain-
bows, waterfalls, may be said to be beautiful in
and of themselves; but how wearisome the world
would be without the vast negative background
upon which these things figure, and which provokes
and stimulates the mind in a way the purely fair
forms do not!

How we are drawn by that which retreats and
hides itself, or gives only glimpses and half views!
Hence the value of trees as a veil to an ugly ornamental house, and the admirable setting they form
to the picturesque habitation I am contemplating.
But the house the heart builds, whether it be cot-
tage or villa, can stand the broad, open light without a screen of any kind. Its neutral gray or
brown tints, its wide projections and deep shadows,
its simple strong lines, its coarse open-air quality,
its ample roof or roofs, blend it with the landscape
wherever it stands. Such a house seems to retreat
into itself, and invites the eye to follow. Its interior warmth and coziness penetrate the walls, and
the eye gathers suggestions of them at every point.

We can miss almost anything else from a building rather than a look of repose. This it must
have. Give it a look of repose, and all else shall
be added. This is the supreme virtue in architecture. Go to the city, walk up and down the principal thoroughfares, and see what an effort many of
the buildings make to stand up! What columns
and arches they put forth where no columns or

arches are needed! There is endless variety of form and line, great activity of iron and stone, when the eye demands simplicity and repose. No broad spaces, no neutral ground. The architect in his search for variety has made his façade bristle with meaningless forms. But now and then the eye is greeted by honest simplicity of structure. Look at that massive front yonder, built of granite blocks, simply one stone top of another from the ground to the roof, with no fuss or flutter about the openings in the walls. How easy, how simple, and what a look of dignity and repose! But probably, the next time we come this way, they will have put hollow metal hoods over the windows, or otherwise marred the ease and dignity of that front.

Doubtless one main source of the pleasure we take in a brick or stone wall over one of wood is just in this element of simplicity and repose; the structure is visible; there is nothing intricate or difficult about it. It is one stone or one brick top of another all the way up; the building makes no effort at all to stand up, but does so in the most natural and inevitable way in the world. In a wooden building the anatomy is more or less hidden; we do not see the sources of its strength. The same is true of a stuccoed or rough-cast building; the eye sees nothing but smooth, expressionless surface.

One great objection to the Mansard roof in the country, now happily nearly gone out of date, is that it fails to give a look of repose. It fails also to give a look of protection. The roof of a building allies it to the open air, and carries the suggestion of shelter as no other part does; and to belittle it, or conceal it, or in any way take from the honest and direct purport of it as the shield, the main matter after all, is not to be allowed. In the city we see only the fronts, the façades of the houses, and the flat and Mansard·are less offensive. But in the country the house is individualized, stands defined, and every vital and necessary part is to be boldly and strongly treated. The Mansard gives to the country house a smart, dapper appearance, and the effect of being perched up and looking about for compliments; such houses seem to be ready to make the military salute as you pass them. Whereas the steep, high roof gives the house a settled, brooding, introverted look. It also furnishes a sort of foil to the rest of the building.

What constitutes the charm to the eye of the old-fashioned country barn but its immense roof, — a slope of gray shingle exposed to the weather like the side of a hill, and by its amplitude suggesting a bounty that warms the heart? Many of the old farmhouses, too, were modeled on the same generous scale, and at a distance little was visible but their great sloping roofs. They covered their inmates as a hen covereth her brood, and are touching pictures of the domestic spirit in its simpler forms.

What is a man's house but his nest, and why should it not be nest-like both outside and in, — coarse, strong, negative in tone externally, and snug

and well-feathered and modeled by the heart within?
Why should he set it on a hill, when he can command a nook under the hill or on its side? Why
should it look like an observatory, when it is a con-
servatory and dormitory?

The domestic spirit is quiet, informal, unceremo-
nious, loves ease, privacy, low tones; loves the
chimney-corner, the old arm-chair, the undress garb,
homely cares, children, simple pleasures, etc.; and
why should it, when it seeks to house itself from
the weather, aim at the formal, the showy, the
architectural, the external, the superfluous? Let
state edifices look stately, but the private dwelling
should express privacy and coziness.

Every man's house is in some sort an effigy of
himself. It is not the snails and shell-fish alone
that excrete their tenements, but man as well.
When you seriously build a house, you make public
proclamation of your taste and manners, or your
want of these. If the domestic instinct is strong
in you, and if you have humility and simplicity,
they will show very plainly in your dwelling; if
you have the opposite of these, false pride or a
petty ambition, or coldness and exclusiveness, they
will show also. A man seldom builds better than he
knows, when he assumes to know anything about it.

I think that, on examination, it will be found
that the main secret of the picturesqueness of more
simple structures, like fences, bridges, sheds, log-
huts, etc., is that the *motive*, the principle of construction, is so open and obvious. No doubt much

might be done to relieve the flatness of our pine-
box houses by more frankness and boldness in this
respect. If the eye could see more fully the necea-
sities of the case, — how the thing stood up and was
held together, that it was not pasteboard, that it
did not need to be anchored against the wind, etc.,
— it would be a relief. Hence the lively pleasure
we feel in what are called "timber-houses," and in
every architectural device by which the anatomy,
the real framework, of the structure, inside or out,
is allowed to show, or made to serve as ornament.
The eye craves lines of strength, evidence of weight
and stability.   But in the wooden house, as usually
treated, these lines are nearly all concealed, the ties
and supports are carefully suppressed, and the eye
must feed on the small, fine lines of the finish.
When the mere outlines of the frame are indicated,
so that the larger spaces appear as panels, it is a
great help; or let any part of the internal economy
show through, and the eye is interested, as the
projection of the chimney-stack in brick or stone
houses, or the separating of the upper from the
main floor by a belt and slight projection, or by
boldly projecting the chamber floor-joist, and letting one story overlap the other.

As I have already said, herein is the main reason
of the picturesqueness of the stone house above all
others.   Every line is a line of strength and necessity.   We see how the mass stands up; how it is
bound and keyed and fortified. The construction
is visible; the corners are locked by header and

stretcher, and are towers of strength; the openings
pierce the walls and reveal their cohesion; every
stone is alive with purpose, and the whole affects
one as a real triumph over Nature, — so much form
and proportion wrested from her grasp. There is
power in stone, and in a less measure in brick; but
wood must be boldly handled not to look frail or
flat. Then unhewn stone has the negative beauty
which is so desirable.

I say, therefore, build of stone by all means, if
you have a natural taste to gratify, and the rockier
your structure looks, the better. All things make
friends with a stone house, — the mosses and lichens,
and vines and birds. It is kindred to the earth
and the elements, and makes itself at home in any
situation.

When I set out to look up a place in the country, I was chiefly intent on finding a few acres of
good fruit land near a large stone-heap. While I
was yet undecided about the land, the discovery of
the stone-heap at a convenient distance, vast piles
of square blocks of all sizes, wedged off the upright strata by the frost during uncounted ages, and
all mottled and colored by the weather, made me
hasten to close the bargain. The large country-seats
in the neighborhood were mainly of brick or pine;
only a few of the early settlers had availed themselves of this beautiful material that lay in such
abundance handy to every man's back door, and in
those cases the stones were nearly buried in white
mortar, as if they were something to be ashamed

of. Truly, the besmeared, beplastered appearance of most stone houses is by no means a part of their beauty. Mortar plays a subordinate part in a structure, and the less we see of it the better.

The proper way to treat the subject is this: as the work progresses, let the wall be got ready for pointing up, but never let the pointing be done, though your masons will be sorely grieved. Let the joints be made close, then scraped out, cut with the trowel, and, while the mortar is yet green, sprinkled with sand. Instead, then, of a white band defining every stone, you have only sharp lines and seams here and there, which give the wall a rocky, natural appearance.

The point of union between the stones, according to my eye, should be a depression, a shadow, and not a raised joint. So that you have closeness and compactness, the face of your wall cannot be too broken or rough. When the rising or setting sun shines athwart it, and brings out the shadows, how powerful and picturesque it looks! It is not in cut or hewn stone to express such majesty. I like the sills and lintels of undressed stone also, — "wild stone," as the old backwoodsman called them, untamed by the hammer or chisel. If the lintels are wide enough, a sort of hood may be formed over the openings by projecting them a few inches.

It seems to me that I built into my house every one of those superb autumn days which I spent in the woods getting out stone. I did not quarry the limestone ledge into blocks any more than I quar-

ried the delicious weather into memories to adorn
my walls.   Every load that was sent home carried
my heart and happiness with it.   The jewels I had
uncovered in the débris, or torn from the ledge in
the morning, I saw in the jambs, or mounted high
on the corners at night.   Every day was filled with
great events.   The woods held unknown treasures.
Those elder giants, frost and rain, had wrought
industriously; now we would unearth from the leaf-
mould an ugly customer, a stone with a ragged
quartz face, or cavernous, and set with rock crystals
like great teeth, or else suggesting a battered and
worm-eaten skull of some old stone dog.   These I
needed a sprinkling of for their quaintness, and to
make the wall a true compendium of the locality.
Then we would unexpectedly strike upon several
loads of beautiful blocks all in a nest; or we would
assault the ledge in a new place with wedge and
bar, and rattle down headers and stretchers that
surpassed any before.   I had to be constantly on
the lookout for corner stone, for mine is a house of
seven corners, and on the strength and dignity of
the corners the beauty of the wall largely depends.
But when you bait your hook with your heart, the
fish always bite.   "The boss is as good as six men
in the woods, getting out stone," flatteringly spoke
up the master-mason.   Certain it is that no such
stone was found as when I headed the search.   The
men saw indifferently with their eyes, but I looked
upon the ground with such desire that I saw what
was beneath the moss and the leaves.   With them

it was hard labor at so much per day, with me it was a passionate pursuit; the enthusiasm of the chase venting itself with the bar and the hammer, and the day was too short for me to tire of the sport.

The stone was exceptionally fine, both in form and color. Sometimes it seemed as if we had struck upon the ruins of some ancient structure, the blocks were so regular and numerous. The ancient stone-cutters, however, had shaped them all to a particular pattern, which was a little off the square; but in bringing them back with the modern pitching-tool the rock face was gained, which is the feature so desirable.

I like a live stone, one upon which time makes an impression, which in the open air assumes a certain tone and mellowness. The stone in my locality surpasses any I have ever seen in this respect. A warm gray is the ruling tint, and a wall built of this stone is of the color of the bowl of the beech-tree, mottled, lively, and full of character.

What should a house of undressed stone be trimmed out with but unpainted wood? Oak, ash, cedar, cherry, maple, — why import pine from Michigan or Maine when nearly all our woods contain plenty of these materials? And now that the planing-mills are so abundant, and really do such admirable work, an ordinary-priced house may be trimmed out mainly in hard wood for nearly the same cost as with pine.

In my case I began at the stump; I viewed the

trees before they were cut, and took a hand in sawing them down and hauling them to the mill. One
bleak winter day I climbed to the top of a mountain to survey a large butternut which some hunters had told me of, and which now, one year later,
I see about me in base and panel as I write. One
thus gets a lively background of interest and reminiscence in his house from the start.

The natural color and grain of the wood give a
richness and simplicity to an interior that no art
can make up for. How the eye loves a genuine
thing; how it delights in the nude beauty of the
wood! A painted surface is a blank, meaningless
surface; but the texture and figure of the wood is
full of expression. It is the principle of construction again appearing in another field. How endless
the variety of figures that appear even in one kind
of wood, and, withal, how modest! The grainers
do not imitate oak. They cannot. Their surface
glares; their oak is only skin-deep; their figures
put nature to shame.

Oak is the wood to start with in trimming a
house. How clear and strong it looks! It is the
master wood. When allowed to season in the log,
it has a richness and ripeness of tone that are delicious. We have many kinds, as rock oak, black
oak, red oak, white oak, — all equally beautiful in
their place. Red oak is the softest, and less liable
to spring. By combining two different kinds, as
red oak and white oak (white oak takes its name
from the external color of the tree, and not from

the color of the wood, which is dark amber color), a most pleasing effect is produced.

Butternut is the softest and most tractable of what are called hard woods, and its hue is eminently warm and mellow. Its figure is pointed and shooting, — a sort of Gothic style in the grain. It makes admirable doors. Western butternut, which can usually be had in the Albany market, makes doors as light as pine, and as little liable to spring. The Western woods are all better than the Eastern for building purposes. They are lighter, coarser, easier worked. They grow easier and thriftier. The traveler through northern Ohio and Indiana sees a wonderful crop of forest trees, tall, uniform, straight as candles, no knots, no gnarls, — all clear, clean timber. The soil is deep and moist, and the trees grow rank and rapid. The chestnut, ash, and butternut grown here work like pine, besides being darker and richer in color than the same woods grown in leaner and more rocky soils. Western black ash is especially beautiful. In connection with our almost bone-white sugar maple for panels, it makes charming doors, — just the thing for chambers, and scarcely more expensive than pine. Of our Eastern woods, red cedar is also good, with its pungent, moth-expelling odor, and should not be neglected. It soon fades, but it is very pleasing, with its hard, solid knots, even then. No doubt some wash might be applied that would preserve its color.

There is a species of birch growing upon our

mountains that makes an admirable finish. It is
usually called red or cherry birch, and it has a long
wave or curl that is found in no other wood. It is
very tough and refractory, and must be securely
fastened. A black ash door, with maple or white
pine panels set in a heavy frame of this red, wavy
birch, is a most pleasing chamber finish. For a
hard-wood floor, in connection with oak or ash, it
is to be preferred to cherry.

Growing alongside of the birch is the soft maple
— the curly species — that must not be overlooked.
It contains light wood and dark wood, as a fowl
contains white meat and dark meat. It is not
unusual to find a tree of this species, the heart of
which will be a rich grayish brown, suggesting, by
something in the tone and texture of it, the rarer
shades of silk, while the outer part is white, and
fine as ivory. I have seen a wainscoting composed
of alternate strips of this light and dark wood from
the same tree that was exquisite, and a great rarity.

The eye soon tires of sharp, violent contrasts.
In general, that which is striking or taking at first
sight is to be avoided in interior finishings or decorations, especially in the main or living rooms. In
halls, a more pronounced style is permissible, and
the contrast of walnut with pine, or maple, or oak
is more endurable. What one wants in his living-
rooms is a quiet, warm tone, and the main secret
of this is dark furniture and hangings, with a dash
of color here and there, and floods of light, — big
windows, and plenty of them. No room can be

cheerful and inviting without plenty of light, and then, if the walls are light too, and the carpets showy, there is a flatness and garishness. The marble mantel-piece, with its senseless vases, and the marble-topped centre-table, add the finishing touch of coldness and stiffness. Marble makes good tombstones, but it is an abomination in a house, either in furniture or in mantels.

There remains only to be added that, after you have had the experience, after the house is finished and you have had a year or two to cool off in (it takes that long), you will probably feel a slight reaction. Or it may be more than that: the scales may fall from your eyes, and you may see that it is not worth while after all to lay so much emphasis on the house, a place to shelter you from the elements, and that you have had only a different but the same unworthy pride as the rest, as if anything was not good enough, and as if manhood was not sufficient to itself without these props.

You will have found, too, that with all your pains you have not built a house, nor can you build one, that just fills the eye and gives the same æsthetic pleasure as does the plain unpainted structure that took no thought of appearances, and that has not one stroke about it foreign to the necessities of the case.

Pride, when it is conscious of itself, is death to the nobly beautiful, whether in dress, manners, equipage, or house-building. The great monumental structures of the Old World show no pride or

vanity, but on the contrary great humility and sin-
gleness of purpose. The Gothic cathedral does not
try to look beautiful; it *is* beautiful from the start,
and entirely serious. London Bridge is a heroic
resolution in stone, and apparently has but one purpose, and that is to carry the paved street with all
its surging masses safely over the river.

Unless, therefore, you have had the rare success
of building without pride, your house will offend
you by and by, and offend others.

Perhaps after one had graduated in this school
and built four or five houses, he would have the
courage to face the problem squarely, and build,
much more plainly and unpretentiously, a low, nest-
ling structure of undressed boards, or unhammered
stone, and be content, like the oyster, with the
roughest of shells without, so that he be sure of
the mother-of-pearl within.

INDEX

CPSIA information can be obtained
at www.ICGtesting.com
Printed in the USA
LVHW081451270322
714529LV00004B/85